D1666876

Benito R. Heyliger is the author of other romance books, including *First Kiss* and *The Chapel Wedding*. Though he lives in Charleston, South Carolina, with his cat and dog, he loves to travel, and has been to six continents, except Antarctica.

Benito R. Heyliger

# ISLAND ROMANCE

AUSTIN MACAULEY PUBLISHERS™
LONDON • CAMBRIDGE • NEW YORK • SHARJAH

**Copyright © Benito R. Heyliger 2022**

**Ordering Information**
Quantity sales: Special discounts are available on quantity purchases by corporations, associations, and others. For details, contact the publisher at the address below.

**Publisher's Cataloguing-in-Publication data**
Heyliger, Benito R.
Island Romance

ISBN 9781643789231 (Paperback)
ISBN 9781643789224 (Hardback)
ISBN 9781645365624 (ePub e-book)

Library of Congress Control Number:2020908430

www.austinmacauley.com/us

First Published 2022
Austin Macauley Publishers LLC
40 Wall Street, 33rd Floor, Suite 3302
New York, NY 10005
USA

mail-usa@austinmacauley.com
+1 (646) 5125767

# Chapter One

Samantha Stamp walked briskly along the hallway with a bit of an extra swing of her waist. She reckoned she was happy, yet trying her best not to be. In fact, she was gleeful. The academic year was coming to an end and in her hands were the examinations papers submitted by her students. The papers were the affirmation that her job for the session was done. And summer was here!

Samantha knew it had been stated that those who couldn't wait to be rid of their jobs in order to go on holidays were those who didn't like their job, to begin with. Here she was excited that the holiday was here but highly opposed to that statement. She loved her job. That was why she was trying to manage her excitement. She walked through the giant doors of the hallway and into a large corridor, and then she was out in the open. The sun-rays fell on her face. She wanted to fling the examination papers into the air, and scream and laugh, and just be silly. She did none of those.

In the sun, her blonde hair was a tad golden and her eyes sky-blue. She always remarked of how different she looked in the summer. She would think of herself as vampiric in the coldest winter and in the summer, she liked to think she came alive. She thought of summer as her own pint of blood.

Samantha was twenty-four, focused, and passionate. She would never use the word 'focused' to qualify herself though. She liked to think she dabbled into stuff, not out of a series of planned moves and actions, but by accident. Only then was she able to evaluate and verify if she liked or disliked the stuff. Perhaps she was being hard on herself but her teaching job was a pure example of how she operated. While still an undergrad, she had volunteered in a supervised teaching program for Arabic refugees and had ended up liking the idea of teaching. She switched courses and ventured into education. She told herself she might regret this as the interest in teaching might wane. But she had been teaching for three years now and was still going strong.

Samantha never thought of herself as beautiful. Perhaps, again, she was just used to being hard on herself. Even after she came to class to meet 'The sexiest teacher alive is SS' scribbled on the white-board, she still didn't buy that. In fact, she argued that being sexy was different from being beautiful. And when she got stared at wherever she went, she just excused them as the 'coquettish glances of drunken men.'

Samantha was walking toward her car, relishing the thought of driving home and having not to bother about reading through a lesson plan or making one, when she heard someone call her name. It was her name, all right, but it was something she didn't want to hear right now. She was even smiling and picturing herself in bed, thinking only of

6

her holiday destination that summer, when she heard his voice.

It was Peter. Peter Clark.

Peter was the mathematics teacher. He was a very efficient teacher. The students loved to see him teach them. But that was where the love ended. Even for the female teachers. Peter had no desirable appeal. He was the bookish teacher, whom Samantha thought his moans in bed would be a quadratic equation or a word problem. This amused her to no end, this naughty thought. And sometimes, when Peter talked to her, she allowed this thought creep in, and Peter thought himself funny when he saw her laugh. He felt encouraged. Samantha always felt sorry for him, as little gestures from her seemed to encourage him. If she greeted him well, he'd send her a note, 'You look incredible.' And if she smiled at him sweetly, he asked to buy her lunch.

Samantha wondered why he couldn't get it. She was just a nice person. She was nice to him; as little as she was to every other person. And each time he asked her, "How about dinner on Saturday?" she found one excuse or the other. She thought some of the excuses were silly but Peter never noticed.

He called her again, "Hey, Samantha!"

The frown on Samantha's face would make a baby cry. But as she turned around to face Peter, there was no trace of it. On her face, was this wide smile, too wide to be true. But Peter never noticed stuff like that.

"Hello, Peter," she said.

"Running off to somewhere?"

"Yes, and quite important."

"Ah! I see."

Samantha thought Peter always said he saw something but he never acted like he had eyes.

"I wanted to congratulate you on a successful academic year... and look, you have your papers right there," Peter said, smiling broadly.

Samantha smiled, too. "It's a good feeling, you know. It's not the easiest job, teaching."

"It is the best job," Peter said. Everyone knew how highly Peter thought of the teaching profession. "And the toughest," he added, "it involves delicateness, conscious plan, and flexibility to allow for the learning needs of different kids."

Samantha nodded. Peter was right. He was always right when it came to academic related issues. But Samantha wanted to be in her car and on her way home already.

"Anything I can do for you, Peter?" she asked, wishing she could do with a little bit patience. She was certain that Peter wanted to stand around and talk all day.

"I was hoping you'd stay a little longer in school," he said. "School tends to be more fun after the exams."

Samantha was surprised Peter could use the word 'fun' in a sentence. He was the stiffest person Samantha knew. Yes, she told herself she was stiff as well but Peter had no competition. Jacqueline, the English teacher, had wanted her to stay, too, but Samantha wanted her privacy and relaxation more.

"Maybe another time, Peter," she said.

From the look on Peter's face, she could tell he knew that there was not going to be another time.

"I know this nice restaurant thirty-eight minutes away. Well, that's thirty-eight minutes from my house, and about twenty-five minutes from yours. On Fridays, tomorrow night, they have this jazz night that I think should be the best in town…"

Samantha was shocked to hear this. Not that jazz was Peter's favorite music; in fact, she'd have been shocked if it was different but the fact that Peter was speaking of the jazz music there being the best in town, like he moved around having fun and eating out. The world was a mysterious place indeed. She waited for Peter to finish speaking.

"So, I think, if you're free, it wouldn't be bad to check it out."

"Are you inviting me on a dinner date?" she asked. In her mind, Samantha was all about, *not again!*

Peter nodded. "I'd be pleased to go on that date with you."

The feeling was not mutual. Samantha cut a regretful posture, her face sad. "Oh, Peter, that's so thoughtful of you. But, you see, I have to grade these papers."

Peter was a little disappointed and this time, it showed. "I could have sworn you have all summer to grade."

"I do have all summer. But all of it is for holiday, Peter."

"Oh!" Peter exclaimed, like he didn't know it was summer. "Where are you going?"

"California. I want all the sun in the world." She laughed, trying to make the conversation as jovial as possible.

"Shouldn't you be heading the other way?"

Samantha stopped laughing and frowned. "What other way?"

"Africa – like Kenya?"

Samantha shook her head. "Come on, Peter!"

Peter looked at her. Samantha could tell he was sad. "I wish you all the fun there is."

"Thank you, Peter."

Peter turned and walked away. Samantha kept looking at him until he disappeared round the corner. She hoped he would, one day, come to the knowledge that she was not into him. She knew the fastest way for him to come to that realization was if she told him, but she feared he may be too bruised. She cared for him as she should for another human. She wished she was a little less nice, maybe she'd have told him to move on, to find someone who would love him. That person was definitely not her.

Samantha got into her car and drove out of the school premises. Once out, her mood, which had been dampened by Peter, realigned with the season. She played music on her car stereo, realizing now that she hadn't played music from the car in over three months. As she drove and sang along the road, a sign board emerged, reading 'Oriental Food Here.' Samantha pulled into the restaurant. "Let's go orient," she said to herself.

She returned to her car fifteen minutes later and drove off. On the passenger seat, was her food in take-out bag. She would treat herself to a full glass of wine from the bottle her mother gave her four months ago, and then she would lie down and think of her holiday. She wouldn't even grade. She'd only bother about that from tomorrow.

Samantha's home was the smallest she had lived in. Even while on welfare, her mother's house had been bigger than hers. But she liked her small room. She liked to think of it like a safe haven. Most time, she'd lie down on the blue mattress, imagining the world in chaos, like an apocalypse had happened or something, and her room being the only safe place a human being could live in. She would imagine looking out through her windows and seeing all the destruction and fumes of poisonous gases and she would fall in love with the room some more. Her bathroom and toilet were just to her side, always loyal. Just against the wall were her work desk and a small, comfortable swivel chair. This was where she wrote her lesson notes and plans and graded students' results. For reading, chatting, and eating, she did while lying or sitting on her bed. There were five pillows on it. At every time, she almost always made use of them all. She called herself Queen Pillows and it made her laugh.

Samantha got into the room and went straight to the answering machine. There were a few messages on it. Her mother wanted to know if she was coming to be with her on the holiday, *Hell no, Mama!*

A school teacher had just called enquire if she would be all right with being added to the planning committee for end-of-session get together, *Hell to the no, please!*

The house caretaker called to say the leaking pipe had been fixed, *Thanks for doing your job.*

One of the messages stood out. It was from Ash, her sister.

Ash's message was hurried. Her voice sounded urgent and needy. 'Sammy, please do call me as soon as you can. I'm in trouble. Please.'

Ash was the mother of all drama. If she wanted to use toilet papers and there was none, she would say the world was ending and that all the toilet papers in the world had been sent to Africa to help save starving children. Once, she had been a little reckless with driving and had hit a guy's vehicle from behind. Ash had no insurance. She could easily have apologized, as the guy seemed like a nice guy. But instead, Ash fainted. Right in the middle of the road, she fainted. Samantha was convinced she was faking it, but when Ash couldn't wake up, the guy got into his car and drove off as speedily as he could. Ash could have chosen to wake up then, but she didn't. She only did open her eyes after Samantha had taken her home and laid her on her bed. She smiled and opened her eyes.

"But you really didn't need to faint this long," Samantha said to her, pissed.

"I saved your ass and that is all I get?" Ash queried her, ever so playfully.

Samantha didn't know how Ash bashing a guy's car had anything to do with her.

"You don't get it?" Ash asked. "We would have been fixing his car with your money."

"Why my money? I didn't bash his car."

Ash shrugged. "I see you'll let me rot in jail, since I have no money. That's great to know."

Samantha felt bad. But that was before she knew how much a manipulator Ash was.

After listening to the message on the phone, Samantha chuckled and put aside the phone. Ash was getting old with her tricks.

The first time Samantha received an emergency call like this one was some six years ago. She was eighteen then and had been working at McDonalds. She usually saved most of her money, as she wanted to make sure she kept herself in school. One evening, just as she returned from work, Ash's call came in. She had just had a convulsion and had been restored, Ash said. She said she was lucky to still be alive and wanted Samantha to come over and get her. Samantha had nearly been traumatized. She hadn't seen anyone convulse before, but she thought it was a dangerous ailment. She went over to the address Ash gave her right away.

It was at the restaurant section of a hotel, The Ibiza. It was a fancy place. Samantha walked in to find Ash eating; her table full with her order. She waved Samantha over. Samantha hurried to her. Ash seemed very all right. Her makeup, her glossed lips, her clothes; everything looked great.

"What's happening?" Samantha asked her, confused.

"Nothing. Could you pay up please?"

Samantha frowned. Ash waved at the waitress to come for her payment. "They have POS, baby," she told Samantha, "I'm sure your cards are here."

"Why do I have to pay for you?" Samantha demanded. "You lied to get me here, it's unfair."

"What's fair?" Ash asked nonchalantly. "You'd have gladly paid to send me to the hospital, wouldn't you?"

It wasn't long before Ash began making a scene, talking about how she was the unlucky child, and how things were designed to go against her. Samantha paid up. Ash asked her to have some fries. Samantha just stormed off. Ash said she was definitely certain she could handle all the food. But it was never going to end there. Ash was inventive. More tricks would surface. If she dedicated her time and craftiness to noble causes, Samantha was sure she'd be successful.

Samantha opened her sealed Chinese food and allowed the smell to fill her nostril. The Chinese had been her favorite chef lately. It used to be the Italians. Their food drove her crazy. Ash had introduced her to Italian food. It was only after she discovered African pepper soup later that she was able to be delivered of her Italian romance. A young African man had been flirting with her and had told her he would blow her mind away. His name was Yinka; she still remembered. He had been from the Yoruba tribe, he told her. He did blow her mind away, all right. First, the pepper had wanted to kill her and she had been upset with Yinka. He simply smiled and told her to keep eating it, that it got better with each spoonful.

Indeed, it got better with each spoonful. She still sipped water after every sip of the soup, but she had to admit, it tasted great. She tried it again two days later. The spice became a lot bearable. "Did they add less spice today?" she had asked Yinka. He said the pepper could never be less; that the cook worked with precision, so the soup tasted the same each time.

Interest in African pepper soup did wane, too, and for a long period, she couldn't tell what she was eating really. But now, there was Chinese food.

As she ate, she wondered if there was any chance Ash could be serious. She didn't think so. She was married, and if she was in trouble, her husband was there for her. She didn't want to be Ash's fool any longer, not after the last straw broke the camel's back.

Samantha occupied her thoughts with her plans. There was the need for her to spend the evening out. The weekend would be her last here before jetting out to California. If only Peter was a great guy, she'd have loved to be at the restaurant he mentioned. The thought of Peter made her wonder why women made the choices they made regarding their partners. She knew a guy like Peter would love a woman blindly, mindlessly, and would stay faithful to her. But women didn't want men like Peter; men who had no-bad boy tendencies, who didn't look great and like they'd tear them up in bed. Women want a bad boy, who was simply faithful. They never get lucky with this. Samantha knew about this. She had been stung. She nearly lost her mind.

Her holiday in California had been a great find. Booked three months ago, she had paid nothing compared to what the current price was. The hotel looked amazing and the food looked nice in the pictures she had seen. The planned locations to explore were great. Samantha thought, for once, life was rewarding her. She couldn't wait to go there. She would take all the photos in the world and would be the envy of her friends. They'd wonder when she came into so much money. Her last holiday in Miami hadn't been all that and she had refrained from showing anyone the photos she took. She feared they'd think she was visiting friends in a low-cost housing estate.

She finished eating her food and put the plate aside. Then she stretched out on her bed, two pillows behind her head, propping her up. "She would go out this evening," she told herself. "Single girls go out, too," she said to no one. If it took the right man a hundred years to come along, should a girl never get to have fun then?

# Chapter Two

Richard Blackwell was wealthy. At thirty-two, he was the CEO of Trans-World Insurance Company, which, Richard knew, would be in the running for the best insurance company in five years' time. Come next year, Trans-World would be quoted in the New York Stock Exchange, he was sure of it. He had put in the necessary works and things were where they should be. Richard Blackwell was excelling in his chosen career like he had always wanted.

But Richard was not a happy man. It was not that he wanted more in life career-wise or that things were taking long to fall into shape, but it was all just because of her. There could never be another explanation. He had tried to relive his life, lying lonely on his bed, thinking, remembering; trying to figure out where exactly his life lost color. His only answer was her.

Sitting up in his dark room, he didn't particularly care for the room lights, he allowed himself to drift off as he thought of her. Yes – Ash; it all started with her. Not exactly, so it all started with Brad.

Brad Pittman had come into Manhattan where Richard lived and had his head office. There had been a lot of business talks, partnerships, and deals analysis. Brad was a financial guru and Richard had made him his chief consultant and as Richard began to expand and continued to consult Brad, it made natural sense that Brad be brought on board as a partner. Brad agreed, seeing that Trans-World had the vision to match his time and input. And indeed, years down the line, both men agreed that it was a wise decision.

Brad had been around and after their hundredth meeting and Brad was due to fly out to New Jersey, he requested that Richard took him out for coffee. It was a weird request, given that Brad was always all about business and if he wanted coffee, he either took one in his hotel room or in the office.

Richard liked that he made the request. It could only mean they were bonding beyond the business space and that Brad was well-pleased with the progress the business was making. Richard took him to Tommy's Place. Tommy's Place was quaint, Richard never really liked the usual. Once he discovered Tommy's Place, he made it his favorite place, and saw to it that he never took coffee elsewhere… Unless he was out of town.

Brad settled in a seat opposite Richard, looking around. "I see why you would bring me here," he said.

"It's a cool place," Richard said. "Tommy, the owner, said he modeled it after a bar he saw in a Mexican movie. I think he didn't make a bad decision."

Brad shook his head. "Away with the distraction, Richard. I see why you would come here."

He was looking over Richard's shoulder at the counter.

Richard followed his gaze. There, staring about non-chalantly, was a lady he had never seen there before. She was beautiful. Richard thought there was fire in her eyes, the way she stared fiercely and confidently. Her hair was blonde, her eyes, blue. They were of the same shade as his. Her high cheek bones gave her an aristocratic persona and her round, small jaw allowed her look innocent and vulnerable. Richard thought she was enticing.

"What?" asked Brad.

"You're freezing?"

"I've never seen her before."

"Well, get ready to thank me."

Brad waved her over.

She came over.

"What's up?" she asked. "You boys want something?"

Richard thought there was something rugged about her. It was sexy. Totally!

"Coffee for me and my boy," Brad said.

She looked Richard over, playing lazily with her eyes, letting him know that she was checking him out. Something tightened around Richard's throat. He wanted to say hi, but couldn't.

She walked away. "Be back."

Brad stared at Richard, laughing. "Richard, what's up? You just froze."

"I didn't."

"Should we ask her? Hey…" Brad pretended to call back the waitress.

"Hey, stop it, Brad," Richard said, flushing.

"Don't be like this man," Brad said. "You can have whatever you want. Most times you forget who you are."

*Most times you forget who you are!*

Richard had forgotten who he was. He wondered, as he sat in the dark, if he was the same person that bothered about nothing but the welfare of his business. He thought of the times he'd sit in the full glare of the lights of his room, researching, writing, calculating, and making presentations… Now he would just return home from work and sit in the dark to think of her. Of how they had lost their way.

Richard had gone back to the coffee shop the very next day. He went alone. He sat in the same place he usually sat and when he looked back at the counter, she was there staring at him. She didn't try to pretend. She didn't look away as their eyes met. Richard looked away. Then he began to think he should have waved her over to bring his coffee, to have an interaction. He turned back again to try and right his wrong but she was there, standing behind him. Richard nearly suffered a heart failure.

"Hey, what's up?" she asked. "Want coffee?"

"Oh, yes, please," Richard said, pleased that he didn't lose his voice this time.

She came around bearing his coffee.

"That was a handsome tip you left yesterday," she said. "If you did that regularly, you'd be very broke."

Richard laughed. He knew she wasn't giving him advice on how to run his life. She was only teasing him into stating his real reason for leaving her such a tip. "My friend left it," Richard said.

"He didn't. If he did, he'd be the one sitting in this seat talking to me."

"And you would know that?" Richard asked, looking up at her.

"I don't know a lot of things, but I know how you boys' minds work."

Richard took a sip of his coffee. It was so good. He smiled. "Your coffee here is special. So, tell me; are you some kind of a bad girl who knows so much about men?"

She looked up at the counter. "Say you stay here another fifteen minutes. My shift is finishing. I'll tell you whatever you want to know."

Richard wondered how his life would have panned out if he didn't stay those fifteen minutes waiting for her, thinking of her, hanging on to the image of her cleavage seen through the split in her shirt. Then, he had thought it was the longest fifteen minutes he had to wait out. But she had taken twenty to finally come to him. She was wearing different clothes then and Richard nearly lost his mind. It clung to her body and thrust her breasts forward.

They talked for an hour. She wasn't the coffee type, so she just sat there talking to him. He couldn't remember if he had asked her out or she, him, but it wasn't so important. He had picked her up the next day after work; they had planned to have dinner. But right in his car, they had both looked at each other with hunger in their eyes and she had said to him, "Drive me home now!"

They both knew she meant his home. Richard drove crazily home. Right there in the car, his penis was pushing hard against his pants. She would later tease him about it, saying she thought the pants were going to tear in two.

They were in each other's arms, kissing, pushing hard against each other, trying to get more than they could, smooching, squeezing, and yanking away their clothes.

20

When Richard wanted to penetrate her, she said to him, "Get behind me." He got behind her and went in forcefully.

She moaned, "Yes!"

Then she said, "Say my name!"

He said, "Ash!"

And they'd both scream repeatedly.

They would have more of that explosive sex. It was the wildest week of Richard's life and he wondered why he had missed out on this for long. She told him she had been working at Tommy's for two months. Secretly, he was glad no other regular customer at Tommy's had snatched her up before he did.

Back then, he wanted to call Brad and thank him for indirectly match-making them. Indeed, it had been Brad who instigated their meeting and his interest. It was him who had left the huge tip and when Richard asked him why, he simply said, "You owe me one, boy. Do not forget to be here tomorrow, so this effort doesn't go to waste."

Looking back now, Richard thought his problems started with Brad. He brought this woman into his life. This woman who now made him sit in the darkness and think of her. He wouldn't say he had ever stopped thinking of her since the first day he met her. But he used to think of her differently then. He would be in a board-room meeting discussing business plans and strategies and, like a rude child, her image would intrude into his space and he would immediately have a hard-on. And he would ring her as soon as he could manage and talk dirty to her, "I can't wait to fuck you and juice all over your body." And she'd tell him, "I can't wait to wear you out and then watch you snore like a child." He would close from work early, and go over to

21

pick her up, and they'd do to each other exactly what they discussed on the phone.

Life was cool.

But Richard was leaving for Aruba. There explosive romance was coming to an end.

"Do you have to leave?" Ash asked him, her face heavy with sadness.

He had known then that she had taken to him. He had to leave, he explained to her. He was relocating his company headquarters to the island, so as to live the life he always wanted, yet run the business he had built. "It's a two-part win situation for me," he said to her.

She wasn't so pleased, he could tell. He thought it would have been a three-part win though, if she was coming, but he couldn't make such proposal to her. He had only known her for a week and a few days and thought it would be rude to yank her away from the life she had always known.

"You've always wanted to live in Aruba, huh? Why's that?" she asked him.

He took a deep breath. "It is a bit of a silly reason though," he said.

"Tell me still."

He sat up in his seat. They had been at a park. It was seven fifteen on his time. Once it got any darker, they would jump on each other and have fast sex. But before then, it was fine to talk. It brought them closer and Richard thought it was a good thing.

"I was given away as a kid," he told her and watched Ash stiffen. "As a result, I didn't get to enjoy the privileges most kids did. I'm just not talking of the shitty wears, which

I got to understand when I was six, was handed down to me and the others from folks who didn't want them any longer. I'm just not talking about the hard bread and eggs I had to eat almost daily. I'm speaking of not knowing what it meant to be on holidays. I mean, in school, when the others discussed holiday destinations their parents had planned for the summer, all I did was hope that no privileged kid asked me where I would be traveling to. They always did." He shook his head. "One day, I looked up this fancy Island on the atlas, and told the other kids that I would be going to Aruba for the holiday. They laughed their head off. They didn't even know where Aruba is, but they just laughed. They knew I could never afford to be on holidays. I had never been so embarrassed." He sat still for a while. To Ash, he cut the image of that poor and lonely kid that was laughed at.

"I told myself I would one day not only visit Aruba for holidays, but also get to live there."

"That day is in the horizon apparently," Ash said.

He nodded.

"I can say you've done well for yourself," she told him and reached out and held his hands.

"Aruba motivated me, Ash," Richard said.

She shared her story with him and he was shocked by how much they had in common. He had been both pained and pleased, and as it got dark, they had made soft love in the corner of the park, instead of the quick fuck they had thought. He wanted to be with her.

Two weeks and two days after they made love for the first time, Ash told him she was pregnant. It had been at the balcony of his apartment; they had been drinking Baileys when she told him. She said it was heavy on her chest and didn't know how he'd take the news. She said she didn't want to destroy what they had and wished the pregnancy didn't happen. She was shocked by how calmly Richard took the news.

"It's all right," he said to her, "I guess this is it then."

"What do you mean?" she asked.

"I mean, I've spent some days wondering how best to ask you if you could abandon your life here and go with me to Aruba, but here the answer lies. You're pregnant. I guess we can get married and travel together to Aruba."

Ash smiled at him. "I can do that. I can abandon my life here for you."

They kissed and he took her from behind, right there. in his balcony. He was pleased she was going with him to Aruba. He envied himself even. A woman as beautiful as she was, was going with him to Aruba. He wished those kids from school were around to see this.

They got married quickly. Richard had no family, so there was none to invite. Ash said her family didn't deserve to witness their happiness, so they, too, were not present. The priest was an old friend of Richard. He tried to spice up their wedding by inviting the church choristers to sing for them. Richard thanked him for his help and took them all out to dinner.

The newlyweds were happy. They made love every day as they counted down to flying to Aruba. Richard envisioned so much happiness for them both. He had bought a good home and had made it the most comfortable place to live in. But his spark and expectations were dampened after two months, when Ash announced that she lost the baby.

*This was the oldest trick in the books!*

Richard knew he had been played. His first resentment of her began only two months after their marriage. She lied to him. And what made it worse was that he couldn't confront her, he had to pretend that he was certain she had been pregnant. Ash cried on losing the baby. Richard despised her tricks, her pretense. From then, he never took her tears seriously.

*And now she was making a damn fool of him all around Aruba!*

He sighed and left his dark room. He was just descending the staircase when the door opened and Ash came in. She was heavily perfumed and the whiff of air from the door announced her entrance before he saw her. Her make-up looked messy, but he wouldn't worry himself with why that was the case. He had seen worse.

As they made to pass each other along the staircase, Ash stopped and said, "Can we talk, Richard?"

Richard grimaced. "About where you're coming from? I'm not interested. Did you even sleep in your room the other night? I don't think so. I've long lost interest."

"It's not always all about you all the time, Richard."

"Which is where the mistake had been all along. It had always been about you and I. Now, it's just going to be about me."

Ash held his arm. "Richard, I can't go on with that divorce."

Richard looked at her like she was silly. "It's done. For me, there is no way out. It took me a while to get here; I am not going back."

"There is something I want you to understand…"

"What's that?"

"I can't explain, Richard, but just understand that we can't go on with that divorce right now."

"You'll get your alimony, Ash. Truly, you will. One million dollars."

"It is not just about the money," Ash shouted.

"What else do you want?" Richard shouted back.

"Sometimes, you need to get over yourself and just understand for once—"

"I'm done trying to understand you, Ash, the cheating, the lies, the manipulations. Fuck all of it!"

He stormed out.

"Fuck you, Richard!" Ash howled after him.

"Fuck you, too!"

Ash came to the open door and howled after him, "Fuck you!"

Richard started his car and drove off. The tires screeched one the stone floor.

"I hope you kill yourself!" Ash howled at the top of her voice.

# Chapter Three

Richard thought of where he went wrong with his marriage to Ash. Even though he had felt she tricked him into marrying her, he didn't think that was the downfall of their marriage. He was going to marry her anyway. He was going to ask her to leave with him to Aruba, and if she had simply told him that only marriage to him would make her go with him, he'd have gone ahead with it.

Now that he thought of it as he drove, he believed their marriage couldn't survive because they had been sex mates and should have kept it at that. They were not in love. When he thought of her, what he remembered was the sex they had. And as they faded away, the sex was no longer interesting. What Richard saw then were the glaring differences between them. They were never the same.

Richard pulled into a drive and hooted madly. He got out of his car and slammed the door. The entrance door of the house, he pulled into opened; a man and a woman stood side-by-side staring at him. Then the man said something like, "I've got this, baby," to his wife and she turned and walked inside.

"Richard?" the man called, as Richard walked to the steps of the apartment.

"Fuck, you look like shit," he added.

Richard walked up to him. He looked tired and angry and sad.

"Let's take a seat here," the man said. "No point bothering Margaret inside."

They sat on the long couch in the porch. The man looked at Richard and said, "You're not going back on your decision?"

Richard nodded. "Yes, Eric."

Eric Marshall was Richard's best friend. When he moved to the island here, Eric had been the only one capable of understanding his personality and temperance. He had met Eric at a multi-national business conference organized on the island. He had been one of the speakers and so had been Eric. Eric's speech had been resounding and he had thought, here was a man he connected with most. He was shocked when, at the end of the conference, Eric had come over and had stretched his hand and said, "Great speech!"

And they had exchanged contacts. He was still stinking, after two days, if it was too early to call when Eric's call came through. He wanted to know if Richard would be available for dinner. Richard was. But they ended up at a bar and not a restaurant. Eric was the regional manager of Arid Bank. He was a man of immense importance and worth. He told Richard to never hesitate to call on him if he wanted an investment into his company. Richard was pleased to hear that.

Their next dinner would be at Eric's house. Richard took Ash with him. Margaret, elegant woman in her early thirties, was waiting with her husband. The two women hugged and hit it off at ones. Margaret was a fashion designer and Ash was a fashion aficionado. It wasn't difficult for them to find something to talk about. While Eric and Richard talked about the stock-market, the two women went into the kitchen to bring out the food. Margaret had cooked the world!

"That's a lot of effort, Margaret," Richard acknowledged, "that we put you through."

"Don't let it make you sweat," Margaret said sweetly, "I had help."

"I will see that I help you clear," Richard promised.

"That will be nice," Ash said, "but Marg and I have unfinished women business to discuss."

They ate noisily. When Eric said something about the stock-market being delicate since last month, Margaret told him to hush up, "If you're not going to speak about the things we understand, darling, don't speak."

"Men can be such insensitive people," Ash said.

"Anything I need to know, Ash?" Richard asked, laughing.

"No, baby, you've been awesome."

Eric looked at Richard seriously. "Be very afraid, man. When Marg says I've been awesome, I will spend the next two hours reliving my past two days trying to figure out where I erred."

"Come on, it's not that bad," Margaret said, laughing.

After they finished eating, Ash helped Margaret do the dishes. "How long have you been married?" she asked Margaret.

"Five years."

"Oh!"

Margaret looked at her. "Go on. Go ahead and ask."

Ash flushed. "Ask what?"

"Go on, ask me."

"Okay. Has there been an issue?"

"No, there hasn't. Not even a miscarriage."

"You're dealing with it all right," Ash said.

"All thanks to Eric. He's been amazing. He hasn't been irrational like most men would. He is working through it with me and he is positive that we will be all right eventually."

Ash smiled. "That's so sweet."

"How about you? How long have you been married?"

"Just months."

"Ah! Young love. It's around this time marriage is the sweetest."

Margaret was right because for Ash and Richard, their marriage, would huff and puff until it was reduced to what they had now. Reduced to Richard sitting languidly on Eric's couch, counting down to his lawyers finalizing the papers and Ash appending her signature.

"I still think you could have tried a little more," Eric said to Richard.

Richard looked at him. "It's so easy for you to say. Margaret didn't cheat on you. In fact, she hasn't looked another man in the eyes. For me, what do I get? A wife who sleeps around; a wife who I haven't touched in the past six months 'cos I can't bear to!"

Eric sighed. He was silent for a long time. "I have a bottle inside, low alcohol content, chilled. Let's see if it can help lighten the weight here."

He went into the apartment. Richard waited.

Eric and Margaret's marriage had been the model for Richard and a few others who knew them. There was understanding and cohesion. And above all, there was love and respect. Ash didn't respect him. If she did, she would not choose not to return to his house at some nights. Margaret would never do that. She had too much integrity to let herself down. Richard wished he had taken time before making the decision to marry Ash. She was wasteful with his money. She was poor at business and was never going to keep a job. She had a lousy attitude. She was wrong for him.

Funny to Richard, Ash wasn't too different from the woman he met at Tommy's Place, but he had been too carried away by the sex. The way she moaned his name when they made love made him feel glorious. Now, he was certain she was moaning and singing other men's names and making them feel glorious. It was a sad life indeed.

Richard returned with the bottle and two glasses. He served them drinks. Richard swallowed his in one gulp.

"We are lucky it's low alcohol," Eric said. He refilled Richard's cup. "This time, sip easy, mate."

Richard let the glass sit. He looked gloomily into the night. "You know, Eric, I tell myself this wouldn't hurt, you know, this thing between Ash and I. I tell myself I'm in control, and that this is just going to pass away. But the truth is, it does hurt seeing her give it to other men. And more importantly, it is distracting. I haven't been able to make a good business decision in two months."

"I should understand this, especially with—" Eric was saying when Richard turned sharply to face him.

"You definitely wouldn't understand this, Eric. You won't. Can you just, for a second, picture Margaret in bed with another man, moaning, trashing about, calling his name? Can you?"

Eric's mouth went dry.

"That's what I thought."

They sat in silence for a long time, taking sips from their glass cups. Eventually, Eric asked, "Is there anything I can do for you, Richard?"

Richard shook his head slowly.

"In that case, Old Sport," Eric said, patting his back. "I will need to go to bed. Have to be at work tomorrow."

Richard checked his time. It was 11:22 p.m.

"I didn't realize how much time I've taken from you."

"It's all right," Eric said, yawning, "I will see you to the car."

Richard drove on the street with his windows down. He contemplated going to sleep in a hotel. But he shoved the thought aside as quickly as it came. The house was his. He wasn't going to leave it for anyone.

# Chapter Four

Samantha's holiday was everything she thought it would be and a little more. The luxury suited her and she remembered that it was the first time she actually tasted luxury. Life was hardly ever great for her and that was why she wanted to enjoy the holiday more. More importantly, she didn't empty her life's savings on this. She would chill by the pool and drink tequila and would regularly dip herself in the pool and splash water. She felt like a child. Her day was most made when a woman, in her early thirties, yelled at her, "You've got that body girl, flaunt it!"

It had been a little embarrassing at the time because the woman had gone ahead and applauded her, drawing the attention of many around the pool. But when Samantha returned to her room, she disrobed and went to stand in front of the mirror. She smiled to herself. When she left the room later, her step had an extra swing to it.

The tour guide also always made Samantha's day. He was a handsome young man of about twenty-five. His beard was the finest Samantha had ever seen. He was Mexican and his accent made Samantha laugh a lot. It wasn't just his accent; it was also with the things he said. He flirted with

Samantha non-stop. His name was Max. He told her, "You do know your bed could be warmer at night, right?"

Samantha faked ignorance. "Oh, the room heater got bad?"

"It's summer, girl, the sun is in your face, so the room heaters are never on," Max said. "I mean your room could be warmer with me in it."

"I suppose that's the line you use for most ladies you guide on tours?"

Max shook his head. "Actually, it's against work ethic to talk this way to a tourist. But right now, I don't care so much. If I wake at home with no job after receiving a sack later, I would smile and say, 'Oh yeah, it was well worth it.'"

"Really? All for a one-night stand?"

"You're not staying just a night."

"I'm just saying," Samantha said.

"Saying you prefer we used my room instead?"

Samantha laughed. "Can you be helped at all?"

Max fell down and faked a faint. "Oh definitely. A kiss can resuscitate me right now."

Samantha laughed and walked away from him. Max took her everywhere.

"You know you should try Mexican food," Max told her. "It's totally amazing."

"Totally?"

"Well, some."

"There are no differences between Mexican food and American food. We are neighbors."

Max laughed. "Tell that to the U.S. government. Anyway, you should try pinto beans and salsa salad. I know where I can take you."

"Okay," Samantha agreed. She thought she was a foodie. Funnily, she had never thought herself a foodie before now.

Max took her to a night club. Samantha realized it was the first time she was going to one since her relationship with O'Brian ended. She was looking forward to it. The lighting at the club was deep blue, so people appeared like alien to her.

Samantha laughed.

"Could you not be close to me?" she said to Max.

"Oh why?" Max asked. "I look hot."

"But you can't afford the drinks here." She laughed. She looked around. "I see some players tonight and I should be having my baby, baby."

"Are you rapping Biggie?"

Samantha laughed. "Move over."

She didn't sit at the club long before two men came over to her table. They looked alike.

"Are you twins?" Samantha asked them.

"No. Just friends."

"Interesting. So?"

"What are you drinking?"

"What are you boys drinking?"

"Ciroc."

"I'm with you."

The twinie-friends ordered two. They filled their glasses and filled Samantha's. They looked interestingly odd to Samantha. They finished their drinks at the same time each time and refilled at the same time. Everything one began saying, the other completed.

"Is there anything about the other you don't know?" Samantha laughed.

The twinie refilled her glass. At the third glass, Samantha's vision began a tad blurry. "Time to dance," she said to them. She wanted to shake the alcohol off her body.

To Samantha's surprise, the two of them joined her on the dance floor. One stayed in her front and the other at her back. After a while, they switched position. The club was loud and hot. Smoke filled the air. And after Samantha was covered in her own sweat, she went back to her seat. The twinie joined her.

They refilled their glasses again. Samantha finished hers and the twinie refilled it, pouring from the two bottles at the same time. Samantha laughed at that. She told herself she might be high and then she told herself she was in control.

"Let me guess, the two of you fuck the same woman."

The twinie nodded.

Samantha laughed. She drank from her glass. "I don't want a threesome."

The twinie refilled her glass.

Samantha saw Max come over to talk to her. She could barely make him out. His head seemed to be vibrating; like it was a particle on a piston engine. She felt him lift her off her seat and she wondered why. All she wanted to do was sit there, finish her drink, and sleep.

The sun's ray was blinding. Samantha opened her eyes. She struggled to force them open. She was in her hotel room and in the same outfit she wore to the club. She wondered how she wound up in that room.

When she saw Max later in the morning after breakfast, she pulled him to one side. "Did you take me to my room last night?"

Max smiled. "You're welcome."

"Why?"

"What do you mean, why? Were you going to go home with that duo clique?"

"What?"

"The duo. Everyone knows them here. The two of them do everything together."

"Oh."

"You're welcome." Max smiled.

Samantha looked at him suspiciously. "Did you?" She indicated her body and Max understood she wanted to know if he had sex with her.

Max frowned. "After carrying you to your room, yes, you crumpled and slept in the lift. There was no strength left to me for sex."

"Oh."

"And then, who sleeps with a sleeping girl, who can't moan?"

"Oh."

"When you can moan, let me know, I will be fit."

Samantha walked away from him. She promised herself she was never going to drink like that again.

It was on the fifth day of her holiday that she ran into Peter. She had been sitting in a reclining chair under the shades of a tree, avoiding direct rays from the sun. Max was nowhere to bug her, so she thought she might as well take a nap. She had been on nothing but her bra and a bum short. Somehow, she felt an overpowering need to open her eyes. Once she did, she nearly had a heart attack. Peter was standing over her, staring at her. She sprang to her feet. Peter smiled sweetly at her. His smile, however, faded when he saw her mood.

"What the hell, Peter?"

Peter stammered. Samantha felt naked. It had been all right to walk around with only her bra, but now, she wished she had her towel with her. She put and arm across her chest.

"What are you doing here?" Samantha demanded.

Peter stammered a little less now. "I'm on holiday. As you are."

"Are you stalking me, Peter?"

Peter looked confused. "Wait. What? Em…"

"Are you fucking stalking me?" Samantha hissed.

"No."

"How did you come here? How did you find me?"

"Em… I just wanted… The holiday…" Peter couldn't finish as sentence.

"Do I need to call the police? How did you come here?"

"You don't need that. We don't need the drama." Peter lost his tardiness. "I saw the holiday website on your phone."

Samantha was alarmed. "You hacked into my phone?"

Peter was horrified. "No! No! I could never do that. I don't know how to hack. I just saw the phone on the table in the office. You didn't close the website and the phone was just there."

Samantha stared at him stonily. "That was how you knew, huh? Why did you follow me here then?"

Peter looked away, as if to find the courage to open up to her. Then he turned back to her. "You couldn't find time to have dinner with me, so I thought, maybe, while on holiday, you could have time for one dinner."

Anger consumed Samantha. "How dare you? Have I tolerated you so much that you had to do this? Couldn't you get the cues? I don't like you, Peter! I'm not into you, and will never be!" Her breast bounced as she talked. She couldn't control herself. "If I needed you, I'd have had you. Can't you get it? You're not a child!"

Samantha was done talking and bumbling away. She never looked back to see it Peter moved away or just stood there. She walked into her hotel room and went straight for the shower. You could think the drama outside was something like dirt and it was now all over her body and needed washing out.

The day turned out to be the hardest for Samantha. She couldn't eat her lunch. Images of Peter standing in front of her, looking expectant, as he narrated why he followed her here, stuck to her. The one that wounded her the most was how Peter stood like a lost child as she berated him. Samantha understood how broken he possibly would be now. She felt sorry for him.

Max found her having lunch.

"You need me to help you with that?" he asked. "You've been on it for thirty minutes and you've hardly had any grain."

Samantha just sighed.

"It's with that man earlier, isn't it?" Max asked her.

"What man?"

"The one you were yelling at."

"Oh, you saw him?"

"I did. I was just coming to bother you when I saw you yelling at him. You passed me without seeing me." He laughed.

Samantha shook her head. The whole event just left her sapped. "Can you find him for me?"

"For a share in your bed, yeah."

"For fifty dollars."

"Deal!" Max rose.

Samantha told him what she wanted him to say to Peter when he found him.

By 7:30 p.m. that evening, Samantha was sitting at The Piazon Restaurant. She was dressed in a black dress and wearing a white pearl necklace. The restaurant was luxurious and the people there were in peers, gentle and loving. Samantha was the odd one out; sitting alone and just waiting.

She feared Peter might not honor the invitation. She had wanted him to meet her for dinner, so she could honor him. She felt too bad for how she treated him that she wanted to make up. When she saw him come in at 7:45, she felt a joy in her heart. She would have her opportunity to apologize and make things right with him. She rose as Peter walked up to her. She offered her cheek to be kissed. Peter kissed it shyly.

"Please sit," she said to him. Peter sat down.

"Thank you for honoring my invitation, Peter."

Peter nodded.

"It means so much to me," she continued, "especially, as I must have turned down six of yours. And you honored mine on the first asking."

"It's all right," Peter allowed.

"Before we proceed to make orders, Peter, I want to tell you that I am so sorry for the things I said to you earlier in the day. They were insensitive and, I dare say, childish."

"I acted like a child, too," Peter said.

"I am sorry."

"We are fine," Peter said.

Samantha looked at him.

"I mean it," Peter said. "We are."

Samantha smiled. "Thank you. We can place our orders now." She waved the waitress over. She turned to Peter. "Just so you know, it's on me."

"No way!" Peter said.

"I'm serious, Peter, I am trying to make up."

"In that case, allow us to split equally."

Samantha looked at him.

"I'm serious. That's how I want to make up."

"Fine."

The waitress came over with a note. They placed their orders.

An hour later, they were leaving The Piazon. Peter asked her, "Wait, what are we now?"

"Friends."

"We cannot be…?"

"We cannot."

"Oh!"

Samantha turned to him. "You need someone who would love you, Peter. I am not that someone."

41

"Thank you for telling me. And thanks for the evening."

Peter seemed fine; Samantha observed. She regretted not telling him she was not into him before now. She had not wanted to hurt him. But she was wrong to have withheld her stance from him.

# Chapter Five

On the flight back to Manhattan, Samantha thought holidays were sad things. They ended. They were usually no Happy Ever-After. There was no point hoping for one. They were like relationships. They hardly ever ended well. She knew. O'Brian had taught her that.

O'Brian was not her first love, so she had not been too love-struck and too much of a child to not know any better. She had been twenty. They met when she was still in school and she had found him intriguing. He was a doctor who rode bikes; a professional who wore jeans and kept his beard prime and proper. Samantha would ask him always, "Shouldn't you have been a music artist?" But that was before he bought a guitar, took Samantha out to a lonely resort, and played and sang to her. Samantha had been blown to bits.

O'Brian was everything. He was the catch of the century. And he was faithful to her.

They went everywhere together. O'Brian would take her to the club on Saturday night and on Sunday morning, he made her bath and go to the Catholic Church close-by with him. He was an interesting human being. When she needed healing, he would sing to her. If it was physical, he prescribed the right drugs. And when he made love to her, she saw the stars. This O'Brian was her soul-mate. He even asked her of her mother and wondered if she needed anything.

Samantha would ask him, "What would you do if she needed something?"

"I'd go over there and get it done for her."

Once, when her mother needed her roof patched, O'Brian surprised Samantha by going to patch it himself. It was that day that Samantha's mother, Rose, asked him to marry her daughter. He had her full consent.

"I haven't proposed to her," O'Brian had said.

Rose laughed. "These kids! I will call her and propose to her myself." And she did call. She told Samantha, "That O'Brian boy, you have to marry him, no kidding!"

"Mum, he hasn't even proposed to me yet."

"These kids," said Rose. "You are frustrating. Well, I'm proposing to you for him."

"What, Mum? Is that even logical?"

"Whatever! Just marry him!"

Samantha wanted to marry him. She knew he was kind and this was more than enough for him. Once they were going to see this movie and he had given up his ticket for a kid who also wanted to see it, but the tickets were sold out. She had asked him, "What do we do now?" and he had replied, "We wait until the kid shows up, to see the joy in his face."

She had thought he was joking; he wasn't. They idled around, played games, and ate ice creams, and when the movie ended, they kid showed up. His face glowed. O'Brian smiled and said, "Now that's all the reimbursement I need."

He had even taught her to be better at treating and caring for others. She wanted to be his wife, because she knew that even if their love dwindled, his kindness would be enough for both of them. But in the end, just like her holiday to California, there was meant to be an end to everything great.

She took a cab home. As she got off the cab, she looked around and said to herself, "We are here again."

She grabbed the mail on her way in. In the cozy enclosure of her small room, she began to look through the mails. She saw one from Richard Blackwell and thought, *Isn't that Ash's husband?* The mail was from Aruba and it had been expressly delivered. From the date, it had been two weeks since the mail arrived. She frowned and wondered what the mail was about. She ripped the envelop open.

She couldn't believe what she saw. It was a letter inviting her to a funeral. Ash's funeral!

It was a joke! And a sick one. Samantha was enraged. How could Ash play this much? This had to be the height of her cheeky ways.

She decided to dial her mother. "Mum?" she said, when the connection was picked up in the other end.

"Hello, Samantha," Rose bellowed. "You're back!"

"Yes, Mum."

"How was it?"

Samantha smiled. "It was the best, Mum. I had a good time."

"I'm happy to hear that. So, are you—"

"Mum, I called you for something. I received a mail from Aruba. Did you receive one, too?"

"No. What did it say?"

"Did you check your mail box, Mum?"

"Sure. I even checked yesterday."

Samantha took a deep breath. "I think Ash is up to some sick joke again."

"What do you mean?"

"I just read a mail from Aruba stating that Ash was dead, and that I was invited to her funeral. Can you imagine?"

Rose remained silent.

"I wonder what she wants to gain with this." Samantha waited for Rose to say something, and when she didn't, Samantha called, "Mum?"

She thought she heard her sobbing. And then the woman spoke.

"It is my fault. It's my fault she turned out that way. I shouldn't have given her away. I shouldn't have. Now look what she is."

Samantha shook her head. Ash had gotten too much pass, just because she was given away. "Mum," she said, "you can't keep blaming yourself all the time. Ash is an adult now. She's twenty-eight! She's not a baby. She should start taking responsibility for her own misdoings."

"Maybe she wouldn't have been this way," Rose insisted.

"She's a grown woman. If she commits a crime now, she would answer for herself. You won't do jail time for her."

Rose was silent for a while. "But it is sad, Samantha."

Samantha agreed. It was indeed sad. Growing up, she dreaded that she had no sibling to play with, and eventually, when she had one, she became a torn in her flesh. Samantha said bye to her mother and wished her well, and because the woman seemed sad, she promised to visit her soon.

Samantha sat back in bed and picked up the invitation paper. On it, was a phone number for the R.S.V.P. Samantha dialed the number. It was picked up by Richard on the second ring. His voice was unappetizing.

"This is Samantha, who is this?"

"Richard."

"May I speak with Ash please?"

"What?"

"Ash, my sister, may I speak with her?"

"Is this some kind of joke?"

"I wonder the same," Samantha said. "When you know Ash, you would wonder. I got an invitation for her funeral and it's just a weird thing—"

"That was a week ago," Richard said, his voice hard.

"A week ago? My sister is dead? She's been buried?"

"Yeah, a week ago," Richard said and hung up.

Samantha was both stunned and angry at the same time. Richard sounded serious and irritated and rude. Samantha was mad at his rudeness and shocked with the possibility that Ash might, indeed, be dead. It was not looking like a trick anymore to her. It broke her and she began to think of Ash's vibrancy and her love for life. Despite all she had been through, she loved life too much to just—just die like that!

She thought now of her sister's phone call to her before she left for California. Ash had been in distress when she made the call. It was making sense now. Samantha had thought Ash was just a good actor. She felt sad now. Maybe if she had returned that call, if she had just dialed her number, she might have been able to save her. Well, maybe not save her, but she would have been able to hear her voice.

She would have had insight into her life and the danger she must have been in. Maybe that was Ash reaching out to her one last time to make up for the years she was nothing but a nuisance to her kid-sister.

Languidly, she walked over to her phone and dialed her mother's number. She wished she didn't have to do this. Rose didn't pick up the phone. Samantha thought it was a good thing. She didn't call back. She hated having to explain to her that her daughter might, indeed, be dead.

The phone rang. Samantha dreaded picking it. But she did. It was her mother calling back.

"Hello, Mum."

"Is everything all right, Samantha?"

Samantha's mouth went dry. She knew telling her mother was the most difficult thing, but she hadn't thought it would be this difficult to form the words. There was no soft way of telling a woman her daughter was dead.

"Samantha?"

"Mum?" She sniffed.

"Are you crying, Samantha?"

"No, Mum."

"What's wrong, Samantha? Talk to me."

"I might have to go to Aruba."

There was silence on the other end. Samantha knew her mother was getting the picture.

"Whatever you do, don't blame yourself over this."

More silence from the other end.

"Mother?"

"I'm here."

"I'm so sorry."

Samantha eventually hung up after a minute of just breathing into the phone with her mother silent on the other end. She was afraid of just packing her backs and leaving. She feared something might go wrong with the woman. She checked the train to Lower Manhattan. There was one to catch in two hours. She packed a small bag and prepared to leave the house.

\*\*\*

Rose was sitting straight with her arms folded in her thighs, when Samantha opened the door and entered. There was smell of dirt and moist in the apartment. Samantha dropped her bag on the floor and walked right up to her Rose and embraced her. It was the longest embrace they ever shared.

"Is it true?" Rose asked, eventually, after they disengaged.

"I think it might be, Mum."

Rose exhaled loudly. "That daughter of mine never found redemption. She lived a troubled life."

Samantha sat beside her. She liked that the woman was talking. If she kept talking, then she'd be fine.

"I see how you cringe that nose of yours, Samantha, the room stinks, doesn't it?" Rose laughed a little. "I haven't cleaned it in days, I'm sorry. I had been having these constant premonitions, you know, like something grave was going to happen. It had been wearing out and I haven't had the energy for chores. I guess, this here is what the premonitions were about."

Samantha didn't know what to say. She opted to make her mother coffee. While Rose sipped the coffee she made, she began to clean the apartment.

"Mum, didn't you say days? Looks like you haven't cleaned for a month." She laughed.

Rose chuckled. "I lose counts."

When Samantha returned to the living room, she found Rose staring at pictures of Ash. It was a collection. Samantha was in some of them.

"Back around the time you two were born, it wasn't so easy to live…"

Samantha knew her mother was going to tell her all over again why she had to give Ash away. She didn't want to hear it now, but she listened. If she wanted her mother to be all right, then she had to allow her moments like this.

Their father, her husband, had died a year after Ash was born. He left nothing but debt for his young family. The mortgage, the medical bills, and no insurance. Worst of them all was that he deposited Hepatitis B Virus in Rose. He had been a promiscuous man. Rose's body didn't react well with the virus. Her liver began to have severe injuries. It was difficult keeping herself in the hospital for effective treatment and looking after two daughters. When the state presented the option of taking the kids away – Ash had been six and Samantha, two – Rose tearfully signed the papers. She insisted on hanging on to Samantha though, as it would be cruel to let such a sweet, little angel live without a mother.

Years later, Rose would seek to reconnect with her daughter, but she was not traceable. The adopter had moved away and had left no clue on how to find them. Rose had been broken. She had tried and failed and had accepted her daughter was lost. She hadn't been Ash at the time, she had been Lara.

It was the daughter who was to find Rose and her kid sister. She returned with baggage and hate and irritation. It was not Rose's sweet Lara who returned, it was Ashley Williams. And she insisted on being called Ashley.

"Fuck that Lara bullshit!" she said to Rose.

It was as if a daughter mad at the world and especially her family, had returned. She didn't want peace and tranquility, she wanted others to feel a part of her pain. Ash never shared what she went through, but one could tell she suffered untold misery. She was resentful of her kids, sister, and the privileges she enjoyed.

"So, you are in college, huh? Aren't you a lucky bastard?" she'd say to Samantha. She had been twenty when she returned and Samantha, sixteen. She was rebellious. She never listened to Rose's advice and Rose couldn't threaten her.

"Do you know what's good about this, Mum?" Ash would say. "You can't send me away twice. You have to live with this."

Rose, with it all, all that Ash brought back, and she suffered. She regretted giving Ash away and insisted she didn't have another choice.

"We all have choices!" Ash would howl. "I could have chosen to die, but I chose not to."

Rose wanted to know what happened to Ash. But Ash would smile and say, "Nothing, I'm fine, can't you see that?"

Ash needed help. But she insisted all she needed was money. To her, money was the only thing that could compensate for the attention she was denied. But Rose was still broke. Ash developed tricks to finagle whatever cash she could from her mother and kid-sister. She seemed fine living that way.

Samantha had, at first, been so pleased she now had a sister. She wanted them to go everywhere together. She liked the fact that they had the same hair and eyes color. It made her think of them as twins. People looked at them twice. They were both slim, busty, and tall. While Ash flaunted the better figure, Samantha represent just fine. But there was going to be no sister-romance between them.

It was almost like Ash wanted Samantha to give her the oxygen she breathed since she hadn't been as privileged. Samantha had never known herself to be privileged. She took up her first jib before she was an adult. She never went on vacations with her mother and definitely, she never lived in a great apartment. That her mother was on welfare spoke volume.

Ash, the sister she longed to have, became the bane of her.

# Chapter Six

It was Friday night. The Parisian Bar was filled with people in a mood that was close to ecstatic as possible. The music was louder than usual and the customers smoked a bit more, so the smoke danced in the air. Richard Blackwell sat with these busy people, but Richard Blackwell was far removed from whatever it was that made them rapturous. He sat sober in his seat; his mind pregnant with his woes. He was on his fifth bottle of beer when Eric walked up to him at his table. Eric had a frustrated look on his face. It was easy to tell his friend's attitude didn't sit well with him.

"Are they helping, the beer?" he asked Richard. He sat down next to him.

"Of course not! Why drown yourself in beer bottle when you can seek healing?"

"I do not need healing," Richard said, finishing the bottle. He began to look around for the waiter.

"That is exactly what you need, my friend, so you can gradually get your life back."

"Not when I feel like I'm responsible for her death." Richard's eyes found and made contact with the waiter and he waved him over.

"What do you mean you feel responsible for her death?" Eric asked. "You're being ridiculous now. She was shot five times, Richard. You didn't do that. You were nowhere near the crime scene even."

Richard informed the waiter to get him another bottle of beer and one for Eric. Eric insisted he wasn't having any.

"Drink with me, Eric," Richard said. "I'm sad, be sad with me."

Eric simply made the waiter go away.

Eric sat up in his chair, shifting closer to Richard. "This is something she might have brought upon herself and it had nothing to do with you."

"The police think otherwise. They have not been able for find any clue that may point to the real killer and since she died by a gun wound, shot five times, and since someone pulled the trigger, I seem to be their easy target."

"That's bullshit!" Eric hissed bitterly. "They have nothing on you."

"You are actually wrong about that."

Eric frowned. "What do you mean?"

The waiter brought Richard's drink over. Richard reached for it. Eric stopped him.

"What do you mean?" he asked him.

"But it is so obvious, Eric. I was getting a divorce. She was entitled to a million dollars alimony. They think I flipped, and just didn't want her to part with that amount. They say there is a motive; that I might have felt bad because she was getting away with all that money that she didn't work for. You see?"

"It's still bullshit!" Eric insisted. "You were willing to part with the money."

Richard eyed the bottle of beer in front of him. He wanted it so badly. Thinking about his predicament hurt him badly. He just wanted to forget, to be rid of the memories and pain of the situation.

"They dare not pin a thing on you," Eric said.

"They could, you know," Richard said. "The neighbors had reported hearing heavy shouts and quarrels between us. Now, the police think I might be violent. They are looking into cases of violent behavior from me."

He laughed and shook his head. "Great country, right? When they want to pin something on you, they find a way to do it. Even if it means resurrecting your dead mother to have her confess how you were a terrible kid."

He laughed.

Eric simply shook his head.

"So, the neighbors had me reported," Richard continued. "Now, guess what I was questioned about earlier today. I was informed that at age ten, I had hit another kid in school. So, they think there might be something there. I remember that incident. The kid had always taunted me and made a mockery of me in the classroom. One day, he pulled at my sweater. It was the best sweater I had. I think the only one. That kid tore that cloth." His voice was low now and he looked serious. "I was sad. I was bitter. I was upset. I couldn't take it. I shoved that kid to the ground. And now, twenty-two years later, they bring it up, and they think it might be prelude to murder."

He reached for his bottle of beer now. Eric didn't try to stop him. Richard gulped half of it down.

"These guys," said Eric, "have they even considered the fact that you loved this woman? That you really were rooting for this marriage?"

Richard didn't answer. He kept sipping his bottle silently. When it became empty, he turned to Eric. "You are wrong, you know. I never loved that woman."

Eric's eyes widened. "What?"

"I'm sorry I had to tell you that. I discovered I didn't love her a long time ago. When the sex became less interesting, I realized I never loved her. And then, when it eventually fizzled out, all we wanted to do was get out of it."

Eric was silent for a long time. Richard thought he looked like a child whose favorite show was switched for a news program on the Television. Eventually, he said, "Well, what's done is done."

"What's done may be done, yes, but it's not the end of it," Richard said. "I will find whoever killed her. I'll start with the mystery lover she was fucking."

Both friends sat quietly for a while.

"You're in no position to drive," Eric said, "I'll take you home."

Richard smiled. "I was counting on that."

As Eric drove him home, Richard put his head out of the window, letting the air rush past his face. This was the exciting part of getting drunk, for him. The air was cold and reinvigorating. And, best of all, it made him forget.

Eric bid him bye and told him to take care of himself when they got to his house. Richard staggered his way in. Drinking had been the better option for him when weighed against exercising. A lot of people had said they exercised when they felt hurt. Richard tried it. It wasn't for him, he found out. Exercise expanded his sorrow. His blood pumped with it. It was terrible.

In his room, he undressed himself and fell into bed. Oblivion engulfed him.

*** 

The knock on the door downstairs was persistent. Richard gradually came awake under the sound. But once he opened his eyes and rolled in bed, he immediately wished he didn't come awake. The headache was searing. He exclaimed and nearly choked in his own breath. It stank like an unclean gutter. The knock came again. Richard quietly stepped out of bed, trying not to aggravate his headache. He threw on his robe over his boxers and went downstairs.

He opened the door to find a sky blue-eyed blonde standing there. He eyes traveled through her body. She looked like his wife. He knew who she was. He was not pleased to see her. He thought she had demonstrated an awkward sense of understanding when he spoke with her on the phone.

"What are you doing here?" he asked her, his voice stiff.

Samantha's mouth went dry. She hadn't expected the door to be answered by a bare-bodied man who looked like he spent a good amount of time at the gym. She had to admit though that he looked wasted. His eyes were slightly dilated and his breath... oh, his breath! He needed, badly, a wash. And that arrogant pose and that voice that was solely unwelcoming; they were not what she expected.

"Who are you please?" she asked.

Richard's face furrowed. "You're standing on my porch. Who the hell are you?"

"I am Samantha, Ashley's sister. I understand she lived here."

Richard only looked at her, a scowl on his face.

"I have questions about her passing," Samantha asked to further elicit an answer from him.

"It's a little too late now," Richard said.

"Please."

Richard's scowl gave way. He just looked at her. He thought she was blinking a little too much now. He knew she was trying to stop herself from crying. He opened the door wider.

"Come in."

He stepped aside for her to come in.

As Samantha passed him, she thought he was quite broad-chested and hard-bodied. He didn't look anything like what she had expected to see here. All she knew was that her sister had married a wealthy man who was as willing as she was to elope. She had thought the man was quite old. What she saw now was shocking. Despite the obvious that he was fighting a hang-over, he looked civil and quite responsible. Ash had always attracted the bad boys, the dangerous men who were as much trouble as Ash was. She wondered what kind of trouble this man was. And if it was this trouble that led to her sister's death.

"I am Richard," he said, pointing Samantha to a seat in the spacious living room.

As Samantha settled on a couch, he asked her to excuse him. "I wasn't counting on anyone and definitely not you calling on me this early. I must go up and dress up properly."

"Okay," Samantha said, looking around.

Eric went up the stairs. Samantha's gaze rested on a particular photo on the wall. She rose and walked over to take a proper look. It was a photo of Richard and Ash scarcely dressed. They looked so happy and seemed not to know when the photo was taken. Samantha couldn't help but feel a pang of jealousy watching the photo. Ash had really been happy, but for her, she hadn't found happiness since. She caught herself over her jealousy. It wasn't right. Ash was dead. She felt guilty.

She really had so many questions for Richard. How could they seem this happy, yet in her time of distress, Ash had chosen to call her instead? Why did he appear so pissed off and not somber? Was she getting ahead of herself? Perhaps she should just try to know him first and hear his story. He was getting dressed, so he wouldn't be long.

In the bathroom upstairs, Richard sat at the base of the toilet seat, vomiting. His hang-over was getting out of hand, he told himself. But he knew the truth. Seeing Ash's younger sister, who looked like her in many ways, had churned his belly. It had left him jaded and his innards cold. Her face brought back memories. Ash had looked that plain. That was before they got married and the heavy makeover and deceit came to the fore.

He felt like leaving the toilet to go lay in bed. But Samantha was here. She had questions and doubts and confusions that must be attended to, and the sooner, the better. He was further thrown into a bad mood when he thought of the fact that Ash's family never cared about her until now. And Ash had told him all about her being given away and then being treated like shit when she dared to return to them. He felt now that it was up to him to be upset on Ash's behalf. They were the reason she turned out the mess that she was and he had been on the receiving end of it all. He concluded he'd let Samantha have a piece of his mind on the matter while he talked to her.

# Chapter Seven

Richard found Samantha staring at one of his wedding photos with Ash, her back turned to him. He watched her for a while. It was easy to mistake her for Ash from his angle, yet she was different. It was like her features took a minimal tone as compared to Ash's. She was looking at the photo, like she was studying it, like she had all the time in the world to do nothing but stare at the photo. She made Richard appreciate the photo a bit more. He had been a cocky son of a gun back then and Ash had been like a blazing fire.

Samantha turned now to find him staring at her. Richard adjusted his position. He was now wearing black pants and a short-sleeved shirt. His hair appeared properly combed now and Samantha thought her instinct had been right when she thought him a gentleman.

"I'd like some coffee now," he said. "Would you like some?"

"Oh yes," Samantha answered.

"Come into the kitchen then."

He led the way.

Samantha stood close to the sink, while Richard got the coffee ready. He poured her a cup and stood to one side to enjoy his. They were quiet all the while. Richard thought Samantha was definitely calm. Even though he knew she had so many issues to resolve, he thought she possessed enough calmness in her spirit to give things the right maturation. She was most definitely different from her sister in this regard. Ash was bubbly and way too impatient.

Richard looked at her sipping her coffee. "Why did you really come here?"

Samantha was taken aback. She wanted to remind him that his sister just died but she understood why he would even ask her that. She cleared her throat. "I thought it was some huge joke from Ash. You should know Ash was good with making bizarre jokes that only she thought funny. I thought…" she broke off. Then she took a deep breath and continued. "I was on a two-week holiday in California. When I returned, the first thing I saw was the mail from you. It was unbelievable at first. With this, you should now understand why our first phone conversation went the way it did. And then when I began to think it could be possible, it shook me. I wished it was a fat joke from her. I prayed it was one of her jokes."

She shook her head somberly.

Richard sipped his tea. "Ironically, her death was a serious thing. She was shot several times."

Samantha gasped. "Oh, no!"

And then tears flooded her eyes. She began to cry.

Richard watched her. He knew he could do nothing about it. He got some tissue and placed it beside her and then he walked away into the living room. He wanted to allow her as much space as necessary to unburden.

It was about five minutes later when she walked into the living room. "Who would do such a thing to her?"

Richard didn't answer.

"I know Ash," Samantha said. "Whatever she may have been involved with, she couldn't have done that to another human being."

"I agree," Richard said. "Her death is a mystery to everyone. The police, however, hold me as a person of interest in this case."

Samantha looked at him with a furrowed face. "Why's that?"

"The old story. When a wife dies, the husband gets asked some questions. However, when they were both going to divorce a week later and the wife was getting a million dollars, you can understand why I should interest the police."

Samantha's eyes widened. "You were getting a divorce?"

She had seen them really happy in the photo and thought they were quite an item.

"Yes, we were. Our marriage was hitting the rock. In fact, I can't tell how we lasted this long."

"Oh no!" Samantha was sad. She went to sit on a couch. Her sister hadn't been happy in her last days on earth. She felt bad. To think that she had almost been jealous!

"It was a bit of a public knowledge, our divorce plan," he told her, "and the thing that led to it was not too hidden either."

Samantha felt he was itching to share why they wanted to divorce. She didn't want to hear it, as she was convinced it was not going to be in her sister's favor.

She made to rise from her seat. "I need to go to the police," she said. And as if needing to explain why she wanted to go to the police, she added, "Ash had given me a distress call three weeks ago."

She saw the interest in his eyes and immediately regretted mentioning this to him. Perhaps, it was safer to keep this information to herself. Richard saw she wasn't going to say more than she had already said. He rose.

"It would be nice to catch up later," he said to her. "We need to speak more."

"All right," Samantha said.

"Can I have your cell number?"

Samantha told him the number. He walked her to the door.

"And you're staying…"

Samantha hesitated. Richard raised an eyebrow.

"Meiz Hotel," she said.

"Good place," he said.

He watched her leave. Then he went into his room to pour himself more coffee. His headache was killing him. His thoughts stayed with Samantha. He wondered what it was that Ash called her to inform her about. He wished she had spilled more. Maybe that information might be just what he needed to find Ash's killer.

# Chapter Eight

The Aruba Police Station was not a big precinct. It would be half of the L.A.P.D. for example, and naturally, handled lesser cases. But it was still a well-run precinct. Police Commander Louis Boyd was a bold and focused man and was quite ambitious. He marshaled his men well and pushed them to be result-oriented.

Samantha made her entrance into the precinct and requested to see the policeman in-charge of her sister's case. It took a little bit of explaining, because she hadn't known if Ash took up Richard's surname or not. Once that was out of the way, she was told to wait, and that an officer would be over to speak to her. It took only five minutes before a lively detective in his mid-thirties walked over to her.

"Good morning, ma'am," he greeted her, "I am Detective Andy Andrew. I am the officer handling Ashley Blackwell's case."

Samantha noticed he was staring at her weirdly and wondered how well he knew her sister when she was alive.

"I am Samantha," she said to him.

"Pleased to meet you. How may I help you?"

Samantha was sure he couldn't get that look on his face.

"Did you know my sister?" she asked him.

"Nope. Well, yeah, I'm handling her case."

"I meant while she was alive."

"No. Never saw her, but I can see a few resemblances."

"She died of gun wound, right? Did it look like an accident? You know, maybe, caught in a crossfire?"

"Nothing like that," the detective said, "it was a well-intentioned murder. Shot from close range. Left six holes in her body."

Samantha shivered. She didn't want to cry. She was struggling not to.

"Did you know she was pregnant?"

Samantha frowned. "Pregnant?"

Richard never mentioned that. What else could he be hiding from her? On her way to the precinct, she had thought of him. He had been too calm and had been economic with the story. And he had been too interested in what she knew. Ash had not even trusted him enough to share the fact that she felt unsafe. Or perhaps, he was the source of such feeling in the first place. If these weren't suspicious enough... She caught herself. It would be too wrong to draw up some false conclusions. Though Richard had said the police were suspicious of him, it was important she based her judgment on facts.

"She was pregnant," the officer repeated.

"Any suspect yet?"

"We have been watching her husband. His motive seems convincing and no clue has pointed to any other person. We've taken neighbor's reports and know that they both had a shouting bout a few times. So..."

"I didn't know that. I just knew they were divorcing."

"What else do you know?"

Samantha exhaled. "My sister called three weeks ago to say she was in trouble. Sadly, I didn't return that call. I didn't take it quite seriously."

"Wish you had."

Samantha felt weak.

"Did she give any hint as to what kind of trouble?"

"No."

Detective Andrew shrugged. "We have carried out a few interviews though. Most of them admitted that your sister had been cheating on her husband and this was the major reason he was divorcing her. So, we can easily liken this to a crime of passion. You know these stuffs get ugly."

Samantha could not take it any longer. She sobbed into her palms. The officer consoled her. Samantha regained her good senses and stopped herself from sobbing.

"I'm sorry about that," she said to him.

"It's all right, I understand. When someone close to you dies—"

"We were not close, sadly."

"Oh!"

"I should go. I hope to be updated if anything develops."

"Sure, sure."

The detective walked her to the exit. "May I know where you are staying?"

Samantha avoided giving him that info.

"I will check in instead," she said to him. But, somehow, she knew he'd know where she was staying if he wanted.

She decided to take a walk around the plaza and the park. She felt depressed. As the details surrounding Ash's death kept getting fed to her, the more she felt sorry for her.

As she walked around the plaza, she noticed people were staring at her. She wished she didn't leave her sun-shade back in the hotel. She imagined Ash walking around the plaza and getting all the attention. Unlike her, she knew Ash would have loved it. She missed her vibrancy. She wished they had been close, perhaps, she might have visited her here.

She felt famished suddenly. It had been an emotionally draining morning, so perhaps a nice meal would help set her right. She looked up one on her phone's google map. There was one fifteen minutes away. She decided to walk to it.

As she walked, she thought of her mother. She knew the woman would call soon. She made a mental note to keep the gruesome part away from her. No mother wanted to hear their daughter was shot six times and no one would love to go to bed with the image of a pregnant woman with holes in her belly.

She walked into the restaurant and ordered salmon, pasta, and coke. From her position close to the window, she thought of how beautiful the city was. Everyone looked happy as they walked by. She saw the women holding lovingly onto their man. She wondered which of them would strangle his wife tonight. She immediately lost appetite in the food.

# Chapter Nine

Richard had to make so many phone calls all day. He had left a lot of businesses that needed his attention unattended and he knew there was only an extent, to which, he would be awaited to bounce back. This Monday, he was back and tackling issues. He could not pin-point to what it was that made him go back to the old him. Perhaps, one of them could be because of Samantha; now that she was here, there were things he needed to work her through.

It was during his lunch break that Daisy, his secretary, reminded him of his dinner with Marta Kilmarnock. Richard had completely forgotten about that.

"I thought you might have forgotten," Daisy said and winked at him. "I have made a slide, which should buttress the bulk of your presentation. After you look at it and there is more to add, I'll be free to get those in."

Richard smiled at her. His life would be messy without her. "Thank you," he said to her, "I will look at this."

Daisy's presentation was perfect. It held the company's figures, expansion rate, and expected returns. It held shares figures, growth, and profit margins. He thought Daisy was the best professional he ever worked with. If she ever mentioned she was quitting, he would triple her salary.

"Send a message to Marta, inform her I look forward to the meeting," Richard informed Daisy.

The Screaming Eagle Restaurant and Lounge was quiet and radiant when Richard pulled up at the park. He walked out of his car and moved briskly toward the entrance. The door-man opened his door, saluting as he did so. Richard allowed him a slight nod of his head as he made his way inside.

Marta was already waiting at their table. She rose and shook hands with him. Marta was a stocks guru. She was thirty-two and already had more than ten years' experience dealing and influencing stocks. Richard was consulting her now that his insurance company was going big time into the stock-market.

Richard sat down and wanted to go straight to business. But not before Marta had condoled with him on losing his wife. Richard thanked her and made his presentations. From it, Marta made her projections and rendered advice.

"Although," she said, "I will come up with exact figures and possible downturns and email them to you. I didn't realize your company was doing this well."

Richard smiled. "We have been smart with expenditures. We even have workers who work from home and only when needed, so we don't have to expend so much on office space."

"That's not enough." Marta stared at him.

Richard laughed. "And I've got a financial guru in Brad Pittman."

"Oh Brad," Marta said romantically, "isn't he the best?"

They ordered then. Richard wanted to keep it light. Marta went heavy. Since they had known each other for quite a while, there was hardly an air of official behavior around them. They joked while they ate.

Marta wondered what men who lost their wives did after they had mourned her.

"I will find out," Richard said. "It shouldn't be an awful lot."

"I wonder if they feel free or lost."

"I should say it usually depends on the relationship they shared."

"I wouldn't ask you how you'd feel," Marta allowed.

"Honestly, I do not know."

"I know. Y'all just drink a lot."

Richard laughed. "You may be right."

"And we know what goes with drinking," Marta teased.

"What?"

"I'm not going to act like the bad one here."

Richard laughed.

***

Samantha had spent the major part of her day in her hotel room. She had declined the services of a room service provider, as she wanted to come to terms with what she now knew about her sister's death. She had spent the day lying in bed and, from time to time, walking to the window to look out at the beach-front, not too far from where she stood. If this was a pleasure trip, then this would have been ideal.

By seven in the evening, she was famished. Having had her appetite messed with earlier in the day, she was now ready for a good meal. She thought of returning to that restaurant for a meal. It was a nice place and the meal had been tasty before she let her imagination wreck it for her. She got up and got into a blue dress and left the apartment.

The weather was nice. She liked the regular breeze that chilled her body. Aruba was a nice place to live in, she concluded. Out around the park, the plaza was different. There were different light here, placed with aesthetics than efficiency in mind. She liked the effort.

She was at the Screaming Eagles Restaurant faster than she did earlier. She thought the distance now might have been halved. The doorman let her in with a salute. The seat she used earlier was now occupied. She sighed and turned to find another. Just around, she saw him – Richard. He had just settled the bill of his dinner with a woman, a bright-faced woman with the body of a model, and they were now getting up. She said something and Richard laughed freely.

Samantha felt bad. Richard had already moved on. Richard, whose wife was only buried two weeks ago, had already moved on. Didn't he try to tell her that Ash was cheating on him? Was he also going to inform her that he too cheated?

She turned and walked away from the restaurant as their eyes met. Richard had looked so stunned. He obviously hadn't expected his dead wife's sister to see him. She could feel the door-man's gaze on her as he hastily opened the door for her. She was angry now. It seemed that the possibility of Richard being responsible for her sister's death was high.

Out in the street, she took left, the opposite direction from where she came. She didn't know why, but it seemed like a good thing to do. When she looked back, she saw

Richard come out of the restaurant, looking around, searching for her. She walked on. Then she began to hear a fast-approaching foot-step. It was Richard.

Samantha quickened her pace and angled off the main street into an alley. At the end of the alley, she turned left. Then right. Then left. When she got into another street, she had no idea where she was. She began to feel she was lost. She checked for her phone to have Google map help her. It was not with her; she had left it in the hotel. People moved around, minding their business. Samantha felt a pang of excitement building up in her.

When she got to another alley, she felt a hand pull her close. She stiffened when she saw it was Richard.

"Stay the fuck away from me!" Samantha hissed.

"I want to explain to you what happened in there. It's not what you think," Richard said.

"Oh, you don't know what I think. Just stay away!"

She broke off his grip and began walking away.

Richard caught up with her. "I've offered to explain. I do not owe you that really. But I'd be pleased, if you listened."

Samantha thought it was the rational thing to do; listen to him. She turned to him. "Okay."

Richard looked around. There were moving people and passing vehicles. "Let's get off this street. Let's take a walk on the beach."

Samantha's face furrowed. She didn't move.

"There are usually people at the beach," Richard explained. "Don't be afraid that I'm going to hurt you, because I am not."

Samantha agreed, "Lead the way."

They walked toward the beach. She thought he was right. There were lovers idling around at every turn on the beach. The beach had been decorated with low lighting, something reminiscent of the light from a full moon. It was beautiful and peaceful and Samantha thought it would be the idle place to walk around with a lover.

"In there," Richard began, "it was not what you think. That was Marta. She is a stock professional and since my business is going into the most important stock-market in the world, I have been working with her to get it right. It was a business meeting and nothing more."

"I understand you were having issues with my sister," Samantha said. "Cheating allegations and whatnot, especially with her guilty. So, I would understand if you buckled and got involved with a woman."

"Despite that, I never was with another woman."

"Hmm."

Richard felt he needed to say more. "I can't say I didn't contemplate it. But I was scared of adding further drama in my life. And so I wanted our divorce finalized, before getting entangled with another woman. I did want the divorce. I wanted it badly I was willing to expend on it. I can't tell why anyone would hurt Ash that way. She had her deceptive ways, so I can't say I know her too well. But this, getting shot that way, was not palatable."

Samantha looked at him. She wanted to see if he was saying the truth. She didn't trust the poor vision from the poor light. She wanted to defend Ash, to fight for her innocence, but she knew it was no use. Ash had the tendency to be deceptive and cheating ran in her blood. She was indefensible.

"Still," she said, "she didn't deserve to die that way."

"I know."

Richard noticed that she was sniffing now. She stopped walking and began to cry. He felt sorry for her. He searched his pocket for a hanky, but found none. He simply just embraced her and tried to make her stop crying.

Richard found out he was hugging her more than he should. He felt awkward about it. More awkward was that she was hanging on to him and sobbing in his chest. His shirt was wet with her tears. Her body was pressed against him. He felt the electricity. His pants was getting bigger in his groin area. He eased her away from him, embarrassed.

"I'm sorry," Samantha said, "I will try to get a hold on myself."

"It's all right." Richard knew he would think a lot about this night.

"You didn't tell me my sister was pregnant," Samantha said once she stopped sobbing. She couldn't tell if Richard was shocked to hear this or not.

"I didn't know she was pregnant when she died. I am not responsible."

"I understand you were quarrelling a lot before the divorce. Was it not because you found out about the pregnancy?"

"Like I said, I didn't know she was pregnant. And our quarrels were sparked by something else. Ash stopped wanting the divorce. It was ridiculous. She wanted me to understand that it was not the right time for that, but I could understand why it was not the right time. We hadn't even slept together in the same room in six months."

Samantha said nothing. They walked in silence for a while.

"Allow me walk you back to your hotel," he told her.

She said nothing. She simply followed his lead. When they got to the hotel, Samantha said she had a request. "Could you show me where my sister is buried please? I'd like to see it."

"I can do that," Richard said to her. "Say I take you there tomorrow myself. Will 10:00 a.m. be fine?"

"It should, except you have work to do."

Richard smiled. "I will see that the boss allows me twenty minutes."

In her hotel room, Samantha took a long shower. She got into bed and fingered her phone, wondering if she was ready to call her mother. She called Peter instead. He was pleased to see her call.

"Could you do me a favor, Peter?"

"This is the first time you're asking," Peter said.

"I will take that as a yes. Peter, please, I will need you to look in on my mother tomorrow please."

"Is she all right?"

"She is. Just that I lost my sister and I'm currently in Aruba. Just pop in for five minutes to check on her please."

"If she doesn't live in India," Peter said. "I hear it's the hardest place to find anyone."

Samantha laughed and gave him Rose's address.

"I'm sorry about your loss," Peter said.

# Chapter Ten

Richard knocked at the door of Room 222 and moments later, it was opened to him. Samantha stood there in a black dress, her face without makeup, and her neck not laced. Richard thought she looked so beautiful and innocent with that plain face.

"Hey," he said to her, "did you catch a good sleep?"

She didn't, so she avoided providing an answer. "I will just pick up my bag and be with you in a moment," she said.

"All right." Richard headed to the elevator. She joined him moments later.

Richard turned the car around and Samantha climbed into the front seat. "It's only about twenty minutes' drive."

"Would there happen to be a flower shop on the way?"

"Sure."

"I'd like to get some. Fresh ones."

Seven minutes later, Richard pulled up in a flower store. Samantha went in and got lilies. He felt a tad guilty. He hadn't even remembered that Ash's grave was without flowers and that was a testimony to how he hated her. But he didn't really hate her. He just couldn't live with her anymore.

The cemetery was lonesome. Richard packed his car near the exit and they both proceeded to walk to Ash's grave. Richard showed her to the grave and walked away. It was a private moment for her and he needed to accord her that.

Richard wondered how it was possible that Samantha and her mother made Ash go through hell. Samantha didn't look the part. Looks, he knew, could be deceptive, but his spirit couldn't help but agree that Samantha was not what Ash portrayed her to be. It would be fifteen minutes before she joined him and he avoided looking at her directly. He didn't want to know if she had been crying again.

When they got into the car, Samantha said, "She didn't like her name Ashley. She preferred Ash."

"I could have that corrected." Richard didn't know why he agreed to do that. "What do you do?"

"I'm a teacher."

"Oh. I hear it's a lot harder to teach kids now, than back in the days."

"I should agree. Expectations are high, yet these kids have the most laissez-faire attitude you'd find on this planet and beyond."

Richard laughed.

"And they get away with most things. Rudeness. Silliness. Write 'Hey, Sexy Samantha' on the white board."

"And they're brutally honest! That should be a crime!" Richard laughed.

"Don't encourage them."

"Yes, ma'am."

"It's depressing. Where do they learn these things from?"

"Do you enjoy teaching?"

"I do."

"What did Ash enjoy most?"

"I can't tell you that."

"Why not?"

"It won't add credit to her C.V."

Richard let it go. "So, how come you never got along with Ash? I can understand if there was friction with your mother, but you—"

"It's a bit of a long story," she said, "though there was a climax. I won't be bothering you with it. Ash felt we owed her plenty, everything, for giving her away. She relates with me like I was there to make the decision."

Richard was quiet for a while. "You two are so different."

"Ash was easily the likeable one."

"From a distance, yeah."

Samantha said nothing. She remembered the several times she was out with Ash and all the boys were hitting on Ash and never her. There was something attractive about her. She was the definition of 'the light in the room.' Even when she chose to be quiet, she still managed to charm everyone.

"Are you hungry?" Richard asked her. "I am dying."

"I think that's one thing I'm convinced I need – food."

"I know where you may like."

"I just want to go to Screaming Eagle. We have unfinished business."

Richard chuckled.

Samantha ordered salmon and pasta and code. Richard chose to have what she was having, too.

While they ate, Richard talked to her about Ash, "You know Ash has an end to end wall of wardrobe filled with clothes. It's incredible. I've thought of sorting the clothes but couldn't go on with it. Do you mind coming over to help with it?"

"A wall of clothes?"

"I'm telling you. I think it's important we sort it out, as there might just be a clue lying around somewhere. If there is anything I want, as much as my business being listed on the New York Stock Exchange, it is finding that mysterious man she was with the night she was murdered."

"Oh. Okay. I guess I can help out with the sorting."

"That will be nice. This salmon is so cool."

"I'd have dreamt about it if I didn't have it now."

Richard laughed. He checked his time. "I will have a meeting in an hour's time. What would your day be like?"

"I will probably just walk around, look around, see a few things. And I might be in to speak with the police."

"I thought you did that yesterday."

"I did."

"Do they have any new info I should know?"

"I wouldn't know."

Richard sensed she didn't trust him. He could not blame her. It would take a while to convince him that he was innocent and as committed as anyone would be toward finding Ash's killer.

Richard paid their bill and bid her bye. Samantha went out to the plaza. She saw a few beautiful dresses and decided to try them out. She wanted some distractions. She was thinking so much about Ash's death, of a strategy to help find the murderer, and this was wearing her out.

As she walked around the plaza, she thought she saw someone dock out of sight, just as she was turning. She frowned and waited. There was no further sign of anyone having been there. She dismissed it and continued window-shopping.

# Chapter Eleven

Samantha was just about to knock on Richard's door when her phone rang. She rummaged in her bag and brought out the phone.

"Hello?" she said hastily.

It was her mother.

"Sammy, dear, did I call at the wrong time?"

"No, Mum, no."

"I have been waiting for your call."

"I should have called. How are you?"

"I'm fine. You sent someone to come check on me."

Samantha had forgotten about Peter. He did her that favor, after all. She thought she should have called him to thank him.

"He is such a nice man," Rose said. "He stayed until I had to shoo him away."

She laughed.

Samantha was pleased to see her mother laugh. It helped her relax. The conversation wouldn't be too awkward after all.

"Hey, Sammy, what's happening?"

"I have spoken with Ash's husband, Richard. And I've also spoken with the police. They assured me that they are working on the case and will find Ash's murderer."

"That's good. Been to her grave yet?"

"Yes."

There was silence from the other end. Samantha waited.

"May her soul find rest," Rose said.

"Amen!"

There was a little more silence.

"What do you think of her husband?"

"I don't know what to think yet, Mum. Maybe, it's early days. But he does seem like a nice guy."

"Oh."

"I'm currently going to his house to sort out Ash's clothes. I hope he reveals himself."

"All right. Just be careful."

"All right, Mum. Bye."

"Bye."

Samantha hung up and knocked on the door. Moments later, it was opened by Richard, who was struggling to get into his shirt. Samantha wondered why he was never found with his clothes on. She took in his physique. It was impressive, she had to admit. She looked away. She wanted to ask him if he walked around the house naked. She felt embarrassed as she caught herself trying to picture him naked.

"Sorry. Come in," Richard said.

Samantha went in. Just then, Richard's phone rang. He picked it and exclaimed. He talked about having forgotten and pleaded that he was sorry and would be on his way at once.

Samantha stood staring at him, waiting for an explanation.

Richard said, "My business colleague, Brad, is coming into town. I totally forgot. Now he is at the airport waiting for me to pick him up. I have to go."

"How about—?"

"I will show you to her room. You'll need to work alone, I'm sorry." Richard was heading up the stairs.

"I'm not doing that."

Richard stopped.

"Maybe, I will come back when you're around."

Richard wanted to say something but stopped. "It's fine. I'm sorry. I will call you."

Samantha left the house. Richard watched her leave. Then he dashed upstairs to get ready to leave the house.

By 7:00 p.m., having been in a meeting with Brad all day, they ended up in a restaurant. They both ordered heavy food.

"I could eat my dad right now," Brad said.

Richard laughed. They drank a few bottles of beer and talked and at 9:00 p.m., Brad retired to his hotel room. Richard didn't feel like just going home to sleep, so he drove around. When he parked his car, he dialed a number and waited for it to be picked on the other end.

"Hello?" a female voice answered.

"Hey, it's me, Richard. Care for a late dinner? Or a night-cap?"

"I'm not really sure I want that," she answered.

"I wanted to ask, you know, like make-up for running off in the morning."

There was a pause at the other end. "Isn't it late?"

"It's 10:00 p.m., this city never sleeps."

"I don't think I can try to find my way to anywhere…"

"I'm parked in front of the hotel."

"Oh!"

It took only twenty minutes and Samantha joined him in the car. They sat in since until Samantha asked, "So?"

"What do you want?"

"I do not want to eat. And certainly, I do not want to drink anything."

"That leaves us with only one option," he said.

"What's that?"

"I will show you."

Richard pulled up into the road. They drove in silence for ten minutes. Then Samantha asked, "Are you driving to the beach?"

"Yes."

Richard pulled up at the beach and they got out. Richard led the way. Samantha followed silently. She noticed that they had left the sand to rocky surfaces. She noticed, too, that they were now ascending a small hill. At the edge of the hill, Richard sat down, and then he motioned Samantha to sit, too. Samantha sat down. She realized the spot was special. Water hit the rock quietly and splashed on her legs. She liked it.

"They say when people say their vows here, their love would live forever."

He took his time in talking. Samantha paid attention.

"I brought Ash here when we first moved to Aruba. I wanted what we had to last forever. It didn't."

Samantha said nothing.

"Love is like death," said Richard. "Wishes have nothing to do with them."

"When did you people stop working for each other?"

Richard sighed. "It has become blurry. I don't know the exact time. It is so sad seeing someone you shared everything about your life with and later, you no longer wanted to respond to her greetings."

He sighed again.

Samantha had no words. She had been there before. She had once shared everything with someone. She had longed for the company of someone and later, she no longer wanted anything to do with that someone.

They spent most of the night gazing at the stars, reminiscing of their individual lives. The water on Samantha's feet was so seductive she didn't want to leave. They sat there until way past midnight. She became sleepy.

"I should take you home," Richard said to her.

He drove her back to the hotel in silence. He bid her good night and informed her to come in the morning to help sort the clothes.

"You're sure you shouldn't go attend to your business."

"I cancelled everything," Richard said. "We will get to work tomorrow."

"See you then."

"Good night."

# Chapter Twelve

Richard was looking fresh when Samantha called on him. It was easy to see he had just shaved and showered. And more importantly, he was putting on some clothes. It was a black body-hugging T-shirt with a V-neck. Samantha thought he looked gorgeous. His pants was loose and his feet, bare.

Samantha entered the room. She was hit with the scent of his after-shave. It was easy to tell he was a classy man. Daily, as she saw and interacted with him, she saw more and more ways he was different from the men Ash dated.

Richard led her to Ash's room. The bed was wide and soft and beautiful. It was a big room. Richard was right, the wardrobe had been from wall to wall. Samantha looked at the bed and imagined Ash wriggling under Richard in a crazy way.

As if following her thought, Richard informed her that the room belonged to Ash alone, and he hadn't been in the same bed with her in six months.

He opened the wardrobe. It was intriguing. Ash had every kind of cloth under the sun. She could easily dress like an Indian woman today and tomorrow, a North Korean. Her make-up section was gorgeous and immense. Samantha imagined her sister changing herself into a human Barbie.

She wanted to ask Richard if he bought her all the things there, but she refrained from it, thinking his answer might force her to dislike Ash. It seemed like he took care of her, all right.

Samantha looked at Ash's shoes section and immediately looked away. It certainly should be a sin for a woman to have that many shoes. She intentionally didn't bother about checking the bags section out.

"Let's start with the clothes," Richard said. "We check for two things. One, for a clue that may help us find Mr. Mysterious and two, for some of the clothes we may want to give away."

"That's fine," Samantha said, overwhelmed.

They began to work. After about thirty minutes, Richard volunteered to go make coffee for two of them. He brought a cup for Samantha ten minutes later. They worked together until eleven, when Richard said he was going to die if he didn't eat then.

"I will make an order," he told Samantha. "What do you want?"

"Italian will be fine."

Richard looked at her. "Just like Ash, huh? She was obsessed with those."

"Actually, my order was to honor her."

Richard regarded her a little. "Let's do that. For Ash."

The food arrived thirty minutes' later. They went into the living room to eat. It was a nice meal. Samantha thought of Ash all through. She went back to Ash's room, but instead of continuing with the work, she stood there looking around. Her sister had been very much alive. Everything in the room pointed to that fact. She loved living. She had made no plans for death.

Samantha became overwhelmed by emotions and sat on the bed crying. Richard found her this way and felt so sorry for her. He reached out and embraced her. She hung on to him, sobbing.

Richard pulled her closer to himself. Then he raised her jaw and kissed her. She kissed him back. They licked each other's tongue and lips and gasped. It became hungrier and passionate. Then, Samantha pulled away. She thought this was wrong and shouldn't be.

"I am so sorry," Richard said, stammering. "I didn't mean to… I am so…"

"It's fine, I have to go." Samantha carried her bag and fled down the stairs.

Before Richard reached the foot of the stairs, she was outside and heading into the street fast.

***

Richard thought meeting up with Eric would bring respite to his soul, so he called him. Eric took the call. "Hey, what's up?"

"Let's meet for lunch."

Eric knew there was something important to discuss, so he didn't hesitate. "Where?"

"Pigmies."

The thing that transpired between him and Samantha had been on his mind since yesterday. He had called her to apologize again, and to ask if he was doing well, but she neglected the calls. Today, all day, he had not been himself.

He kept telling himself Samantha had forgiven him and that all will be as normal, but he was not convinced. He had to talk to someone about it and Eric was the man.

They met at the Pigmies. While Eric ate his food with zeal and purpose, Richard nibbled his. He was distracted. Eric finished his food and wiped his mouth clean.

"Tell me what it is. You are clearly bothered."

"I think I messed up," Richard said.

"Tell me."

"I kissed Samantha. Samantha is Ash's younger sister…"

Eric's jaw dropped. "You what?"

"I—it just happened. None of us worked to make it happen."

"You are a crazy man." Eric said that slowly and it tended to have more effect that way. And then his voice came hard, "You don't behave that way! It's just a month now after Ash's death."

"You seem mad at me," Richard said. "I do not owe that woman the respect of time, I could be in a relationship whenever I want. I admit I do not want that relationship to be with her sister, but I can't help the attraction."

"It's every shade of wrong, Richard. When it blows up in your face, don't say I didn't warn you about—"

Eric noticed Richard had frozen and was now looking ahead of him. There was a woman standing there. Eric knew who she was right away – Samantha. He wondered if Richard invited her here.

Richard beckoned at her to come over. He knew, from the way she stood flushed, that she was thinking about the kiss yesterday. He hated this situation he had put her in. He wanted to make amends.

Samantha came over reluctantly.

"Hey, Samantha, here is my good friend, Eric…" Richard said. "And Eric…"

He turned to Eric to introduce him to Samantha. But Eric rose at once.

"I was just leaving Samantha," he said. "Do take care."

Richard's mouth went dry. He stared as Eric left, surprised. He turned back to Samantha. "Please take a seat, Samantha."

She did, sitting in front of him. They stared at each other and then looked away. The silence lingered. Then Richard spoke up, "It was a foolish thing I did in that room. I am definitely sorry about—"

He realized now that Samantha too had been talking. She was apologizing at the same time. Richard thought it was good. It meant they would put this behind them quickly.

"You're here for lunch," Richard said. "I'll get the waiter."

"No, do not bother about that. You are already done. I'll get the waiter after you're gone."

Richard understood Samantha still felt awkward around him, despite their being sorry. He would have to live with that for a few days.

"How long are you staying?" he asked her. "I mean in Aruba."

"I have all summer. Though, the hotel bills are crazy."

Richard nodded. Aruba was quite an expensive place to lodge in.

"I could leave anytime, but I would love to not leave without a tangible piece of progress from the police."

"True that," Richard said, "I don't know how much more money you have. But given you already vacationed in California and now Aruba, you won't have a huge stark in your account. I suggest you move into the guest-room in the house."

Samantha frowned. "Your house?"

"What? You have a better option?"

Samantha thought about it. Indeed there weren't a lot of options left. She was financially exhausted. And if she wanted to see the end or at least tangible progress with Ash's case, she needed to spend more time here.

She nodded to Richard. "Thanks for the offer. I will take it."

"All right." Richard rose. "I will be over at the hotel in the evening after work to pick you up. Enjoy your meal."

"Bye."

# Chapter Thirteen

Samantha hadn't had peace of mind all day. She was concerned with the thought of moving into her dead sister's home. She wondered if it was worth it. If she packed up and left Aruba now, would she be haunted with the thoughts of not helping her sister find justice? She had clearly been brutally murdered and the culprit didn't deserve to be walking free. She reluctantly packed her things and waited for Richard.

At 7:30 a.m., he was yet to show up. She wondered if he had decided not to follow through with his words. Perhaps, he thought it was a foolish idea.

Her room phone rang at 7:37 p.m. and the receptionist informed her that a man was waiting for her. She left her room to the reception. She wondered why Richard wouldn't come up to her room like he did the first time he came here. She thought maybe he just wanted to talk, so she left her things in her room and went down to the reception.

The receptionist pointed outside to the hotel's first lobby. "He's there."

Samantha went to the lobby that led to the hotel's exit. He was standing there all right, facing away from her.

Samantha walked over to him. She was convinced he had changed his mind.

"Hello, Samantha."

It was not Richard. It was O'Brian standing there. Samantha frowned.

"You look well," he said.

"What are you doing here, O'Brian?"

"I came to see you. A lot has happened and a lot has changed. I thought we could finally relax and talk about us."

"Why should we do that?"

O'Brian walked closer to her calmly and assuredly. "I have not found another woman I could love. I am convinced you're the only woman for me."

Samantha shook her head. "You said that before, didn't you?"

"I did. And now, three years later, I don't feel any different."

Samantha looked at him and shook her head. "Did you know a former U.S. President apologized to all the black people for the white man's terrible act in enslaving them years ago? Oh, yes! Was that meant to placate the black people? Yes. Did it? No. It's never enough. Nothing can be enough. Sometimes, that's usually the case. Nothing can just be enough. That is the case of you and I."

"Come on, Samantha, I understand why you had to give me this history lesson. I get it. But if you look around, black and white people live together, believe in America, and would certainly not want to be anywhere else."

"That's because the black man and the white man were never brothers. They can afford not to take each other's sin to heart."

O'Brian was quiet for a while. "Can you afford not to take my sin to heart, Samantha?"

"You slept with my sister!" Samantha hissed.

O'Brian felt tired. Samantha stared at him; face furrowed with anger.

"How dare you show up here again?"

"Samantha, your sister wanted to ruin us. She wanted to ruin your happiness. You let her succeed…"

Samantha was mad now. "I let her succeed? How dare you say that? How dare you even make an attempt to put it on me? You were the one in bed with her!"

O'Brian waited for Samantha to calm down before speaking. "I think I was a pawn in that matter and would have ended up in her bed, no matter what I did. I feel like I was the victim in that whole ploy."

"Oh, you were the victim? Can you listen to yourself? Can you, O'Brian? You were moaning and clearly enjoying yourself when I found you."

"It was sex, Samantha. I wasn't getting killed."

"And there would have been more episodes of that, if you didn't get caught, wouldn't there? My sister was clearly good. You'd have gone back for more."

O'Brian had no answer. He stood there for two minutes without saying a word. Samantha wanted to walk back to her room, but she wanted to do that only after she was certain O'Brian was gone.

"Ashley wanted us to be unhappy," O'Brian said. "Now that she is gone, can we find that happiness?"

Samantha frowned. "What did you say?"

O'Brian remained quiet.

"You know about her death? How did you know that?"

"That's not hard to know."

"How the hell did you know about her death?"

O'Brian looked at her for a while. "Come with me, I'll show you something."

He turned and began walking out of the lobby. Samantha hesitated. O'Brian didn't turn his back to see if she was following. It was like he knew she had no other option. He was right. Samantha followed after him.

O'Brian walked to the parked in the hotel premise and got in. He opened the passenger door to Samantha. She stood there not getting in.

"Where are you taking me to, O'Brian?"

"You wanted to know things, didn't you?"

Samantha just stood there. She was meant to wait for Richard. But he hadn't even call her. He probably was never going to call. Here was a chance to find out something no one seemed to know about Ash. She got into the car. She was taking it.

They drove for ten minutes in silence. Samantha asked, "So, where have you been living all this while?"

"I move around a lot. I stopped working at the hospital and became a consultant. This way, I was never tired down in a place. I joined a band and we toured everywhere."

"I see you're living your dream."

O'Brian remained quiet.

"You're the lead singer?"

"No, I'm not good enough."

"You're not?"

O'Brian remained quiet. After five minutes, he spoke again, "Touring with a band was not the dream. The dream was to live with you. To be married to you. That was the dream. Sadly, it became clearer after we parted ways."

It was Samantha's turn to remain quiet.

O'Brian pulled away from the road and angled toward the beach. They would be on this path for another ten minutes before he pulled up at a lonely beach house.

"Where is this place?" Samantha asked.

"It's my house." O'Brian got out of the car and nodded to Samantha to do the same. Samantha had the wrong premonition about this place, it was dark and lonesome. She got out and followed him. She told herself she'd bolt if she sensed anything strange.

O'Brian opened to door and got it. It was so dark inside, so Samantha chose to remain outside. O'Brian chuckled and turned the light one. The room was wide and long. It had everything anyone needed to survive in it. There were two couches, a small bed, a work table, a kitchen in one corner, cameras, and a sound and video display system.

"What is this place?" Samantha asked.

"I told you."

She went inside. O'Brian closed the door.

"Why did you bring me here?"

"I thought we both know that."

"Why?"

"To work toward being happy."

"What the hell?"

O'Brian chuckled. "Relax. God, Samantha, what has gotten into you?"

Samantha inhaled deeply, but she couldn't relax.

O'Brian turned on a computer. He waited for it to come on. Once it was on, he began displaying images on the monitor. They were photos of him with different women. There were fifteen in all.

"These are the women I've been with in the time since we separated. I have seen them all. I don't want to be with any of them. I want to be with only one. And she is standing right here in this room."

Samantha frowned. "I didn't come here for this shit!"

"I know. We will get to why you are here. You see, Samantha, in the time that I have been with these fifteen women, you have been with three men..."

Samantha looked at him, shocked.

"Jamie. Henry, and Martins. You couldn't bring yourself to love any of them. You never lasted with any of them. Why?"

"You've been stalking me?"

"I have been doing a little more than that, honey. I have been making money, too, building a future for us. You see, I'm not hopeless."

Samantha couldn't believe what she was hearing. "You were never like this! You were never obsessed, O'Brian."

"I guess I didn't know who I was."

"You used to be very assured, competent, and contented."

"I wouldn't say I'm not. Only, in addition to those, I want you."

It dawned on Samantha now. What she saw at the plaza wasn't a figment of her own imagination. It was O'Brian. He had been stalking her.

"You're crazy!" she said to him.

"You will miss the good part, if you don't calm down. To show you I have been putting in the works for us to be back, I met your sister Ash."

Samantha's gaze narrowed.

"I met her a month before she died…"

Samantha wondered if O'Brian was the secret lover Richard had been referring to.

"But the truth is she was just meeting me. I had been meeting her as often as I wanted. And boy, did she have an interesting life?"

Samantha wished she could reach out and smack him hard.

"Anyway, I met her. I told her she owed me one thing; to repair what she ruined. I told her she must get you and I back together. She knew I was not kidding."

"What did you threaten her with?"

"Threat? I didn't threaten her."

"You simple told her what to do and she agreed with you?"

"Yes. Although I think a few photos I showed her from my memory card might have helped persuade her."

"You showed her photos of her and the men she was cheating with?"

"Bingo! You got that right. She feared I might publicize them. So, she vowed to work hard to bring us back together."

"So, at what point did you decide you didn't need her help any longer and chose to kill her?"

O'Brian snorted. "I didn't kill her."

"Yeah, tell that to the police!"

Samantha stormed out. She walked to the door and turned the handle. It didn't turn. She couldn't open the door. She turned back to O'Brian, who hadn't moved a muscle since.

"Let me out!"

"So you can run to the police and tell them how I am responsible? Are you foolish? Do you have evidence?"

"The police will find it."

"Everyone believes the police are righteous and that the police would help them." He laughed. "The police are not innocent."

He began to walk gradually toward where Samantha stood.

"Get away from me!" Samantha shouted.

"No," said O'Brian, "as a matter of fact, I'm just going to grab you and bundle you into a chair."

Samantha was horrified. "Let me go!"

O'Brian continued like he hadn't been interrupted, "And then I will talk to you until you gain some sense. This won't take beyond a week, I'm sure."

"What?"

O'Brian grabbed her and dragged her to a seat. "Plant yourself in here. Don't try to walk around. Plants don't walk."

"Why are you doing this?"

"I'm famished. Let me find something to eat and afterwards, I will answer you."

He walked to his mini kitchen and turned the gas on. "I want to make oats. Want some?"

Samantha remained quiet.

"That's what I thought." He proceeded to make oats. Then he got chicken wings from the fridge and carried it to the seat in front of Samantha. He ate greedily. Samantha thought he was so different from the man she knew. O'Brian was a classy man. This here was a damaged man.

When he was done eating, he carried the plate to the sink and washed them. Then he arranged them back in their rack. Samantha was so confused staring at him. Then he returned to his seat in front of Samantha.

"Now, where were we?" he asked. "Oh, I remember. Me, you, and Ash. So I asked Ash to do this little thing for me and she promised to get it done. She swore she was capable of doing it. What I couldn't understand was why she was taking long. Anyway, she finally gave me her word that she was making progress with you. I said I wanted to meet up and discuss. The night we were meant to meet up was the night she died."

It took Samantha a few seconds before she said, "And this is meant to exonerate you, huh? I mean, with this, I'm to go home believing you had nothing to do with her death?"

"I have no reason to lie to you. In fact, I have no reason to share these stories with you. I was the one who found you."

"Actually, you do have a reason. You wanted to make me see you are still in love with me, that we are meant to be together. And at the same time, you wanted me to see the effort you were making and willing to make to bring us back together. Anyway, I don't see it. I can never be with you. You have, in fact, fallen off the radar for me."

"That's sad." O'Brian cut the figure of a depressed man.

Samantha thought he had added acting to his list of talents.

"What do you plan to do with me?" she asked him. "You have the door locked. You told me to not move. You intend to talk to me until I agree to be back with you…"

"I don't want you to agree to be back with me, Samantha. I want you to see why you should be back with me."

"We can sit here as long as we want. We won't achieve that. So, you might as well let me go."

"Oh dear, you are going nowhere."

"Have I been abducted?"

"Don't be dramatic, Samantha. Tell me, how is your mum?"

"She would be pleased to hear of this day."

"Let's make love, Samantha."

"What?" Samantha was horrified.

"Come on, don't be too shocked. It will help us recapture our love."

"No, thanks." Samantha tried to sound brave. But she was terrified now. This O'Brian was capable of anything.

"Wait, you don't have your phone with you, do you?"

Samantha said nothing. O'Brian rose and went over to her. He frisked her and found her phone with her. There were more than twenty missed calls showing on the screen. The GPS had been active. O'Brian was mad.

"You tricked me!"

"How?"

"You set your GPS tracking up."

"I'm in a place I don't know, so I keep it open. It was never because of you. I bet I still thought you were a sane guy."

O'Brian was no longer paying attention to her. He went over to his computer and began configuring something fast.

"If anyone comes here because of your tracking, they'd find nothing on me. A tap of this button and all in this system is formatted."

They heard it at the same time. A loud knock on the door. O'Brian shook visibly.

"You are busted!" Samantha said.

O'Brian went to look at the door through the window. There were two men standing there. One of them was muscular and looked like a police detective. The other was Ash's husband. He went back to the computer and tapped the button. The system, in seconds, went blank.

O'Brian went to open the door.

Richard stared at him sternly. "We are looking for a young lady around here. Did you see anyone?"

"Oh yeah, she was just leaving."

"What?"

O'Brian called out to Samantha. Samantha went to the door. She saw Richard and a strange man. She quickly went over to Richard and collapsed into his arms.

Richard led her away from the house. "What happened?"

"Get my phone from him please."

Richard nodded to Brad. Brad went over to the house. O'Brian was still standing there. He stretched out his hand and handed Brad the phone. Brad scowled at him before leaving. When he got to Richard, he was dialing 911.

# Chapter Fourteen

"The company was at a risk of not getting into the New York Stock Exchange listing," Marta called Richard to inform him. After critically going through the company's financial document, she pointed out a few irregularities that needed to be worked on. This had set Richard and Brad on their toes and they were at it until late evening. Brad was scheduled to leave the next morning, so it was paramount they completed their task.

He thought he should have called Samantha to inform her he was going to be at the hotel late but he hadn't even told her when he would be coming. He figured he could be excused. By 7:55 p.m., when he eventually got to her room, she was not there. He called her, but she wouldn't pick up.

Downstairs at the reception hall, the receptionist told him Samantha was at the lobby to meet a man. Samantha was not at the lobby. She was not anywhere in sight. He dialed her number again. She didn't take it. He went back to the receptionist to find out if she knew who the man was. She didn't. And she couldn't describe him, except that the man was tall.

"Just great," Richard said. He waited another ten minutes, dialing Samantha's number every two minutes.

Then he went back to the receptionist and insisted she checked the room. A room-service provider was called upon to check Samantha's room. Samantha was not in her room. Richard began to panic.

After another ten minutes, he insisted that the hotel did something. Perhaps, check their CCTV footages to see whom it was that Samantha had been with.

"But the lobby is not wired with camera," Richard was told.

"She just can't be gone like that and all we have to do is wait."

"What should we do?"

"Maybe get the police involved?"

The receptionist laughed. "They can't do anything. She's only been gone thirty minutes."

"She's not from here. The earlier we began to look, the better for her."

"Would you know where she goes to?" the receptionist asked.

"I know a restaurant. But she couldn't have gone there, I was meant to take her to dinner."

The receptionist didn't know what to do. Richard suggested they went into Samantha's and used her laptop to track her phone.

"But I can't let you do that, sir."

"Don't let me. I don't want to do it even. But you have tech guys here, I'm sure they can help. This hotel owes it to her to help keep her safe."

The receptionist hesitated.

"I know you do not know me and think you don't have to do anything I want. She is my wife's sister and I would take this personal if anything happens to her."

Samantha's phone was tracked all right. It was easy. Her laptop played a huge role. Her phone was registered in her Google account and with the phone's GPS turned on, her whereabouts was located.

Richard took off. He couldn't understand why Samantha would be the end of the beach twenty-five minutes from where her hotel was. He called Brad on his way and told him to get ready for a little ride.

He explained the process of finding her and Samantha was pleased that he went through the trouble. When he dialed the police, they promised to be there in ten minutes. The police took eighteen minutes. When they got there, O'Brian was not in the house. Samantha found him on Facebook and gave the police his photos.

They assured Samantha that they'd find O'Brian in no time. She was also informed to report at the station the next day, "We will need you to recount your report and to see if anything new comes up."

Richard took her home after getting her things from the hotel. He led her to the guest room and made her relax.

"I want you to feel fine," he said to her. "I am just a phone call away."

"Don't forget to catch some sleep," Samantha said.

"You, too."

The next morning, before Richard left for work, he slipped under the door for Samantha. Samantha found it. Richard wanted to let her know that there was coffee and sandwich in the kitchen and that he'd be looking to have dinner with her, if she was up to it.

O'Brian got arrested in the wee hours of the morning. Samantha was informed when she showed up at the police station. The police said they'd charge him with deceit and attempted abduction. However, they wished they had evidence of the other allegations of stalking and blackmailing her sister.

"But he did all that," said Samantha. "He's obsessed."

"We found nothing to that effect."

"He wiped his computer clean."

"We can't do anything about that."

"Just keep him away from me."

"You bet, we will."

Detective Andrew wanted to take Samantha out to dinner, he told her. "I am the soul of this city, like its moral compass," he said, "but I will make time if you agreed to one dinner with me."

"It's no use, sir," Samantha said, "I will be leaving soon anyway."

"Em, to Venus?"

"Very funny," Samantha said, not laughing. "Has your department made any progress?"

"Not until you helped us arrest this man, O'Brian. Seems like we are going to find him useful."

"I'm glad."

Just before she left, the detective implored her to consider that dinner. Samantha promised she wouldn't. She didn't tell him this anyway.

On her way home, she contemplated Richard's offer to dinner. She thought her life needed the relaxation only a nice dinner could offer. She thought of what to wear and decided it would be best to keep it simple.

She took her time to shower. She had just finished preening herself in front of the mirror when Richard knocked.

"Open," Samantha said.

Richard opened the door. He gasped noticeably on seeing her. A short, white dress, and a simple necklace did it for her.

"You look lovely," he said to her.

"Thank you."

"Here." He showed her a coat. "This is Ash's. I found it in her things. I think you should keep it."

"Oh, thanks." Samantha felt pleased to have something that belonged to her sister. She placed it on the bed.

"Ready?" Richard asked.

"Yes."

"Right. Let's go."

They went to Barefoot Restaurant. It was a lovely place. Samantha immediately preferred it to the Screaming Eagle. They placed their order.

"I can totally understand why you would want to live here, Richard," she said. "It's such a lovely place. And peaceful. And the temperature, cool."

"I wanted to live here a long time ago," Richard said, "and moving over here with Ash was a dream come true for me at the time. I grew up with a family. I was raised by the state. Ash shared her story with me; she didn't have a family, too. I thought we shared that in common, and therefore, wanted the same thing; a family. So when she told me she was pregnant, I was so happy. I thought to myself,

*I'm finally going to have a family*. It was the happiest time of my life. And I was moving to my favorite city. But Ash…" He shook his head. "She was not pregnant. She only told me that to be married to me."

Samantha shook her head. "I feel sad for you."

Their orders arrived. Samantha swallowed hard, smiling.

"What's the saddest thing Ash made you go through, Samantha? You two never got along, so I know something grave must have gone down."

Samantha sighed, pausing from forking her food.

"O'Brian was going to be my husband. We were only six days away from tying the knot." She chuckled. "We were so in love. You should have seen him three years ago. The real stud. He could do everything. I wanted to be like him. He motivated me. I found him in bed with my sister."

Richard gasped.

Samantha chuckled. "It was easy to see that my sister engineered it all. Because, in the end, she told me it was great I found out about it before it was too late."

Richard dropped his spoon. "She never told me this. She made it appear like her family, you and your mother, were monsters."

"Most times I wish things were different for her."

"She did go through things while she was away from home," Richard said. "Sadly, she didn't share those things with me. She got messed up and, in the end, it isn't her fault."

Samantha stopped eating. She looked somber.

"I think we should stop talking about Ash now."

"I agree. We need to enjoy our dinner."

They ate in silence. When the waiter came around, so they could order desert, Samantha asked for their sweetest cake.

After dinner, Richard said to her, "Let's not be too quick to go back to the house. You haven't seen the Lighthouse, have you?"

"I'd be pleased to see it."

Richard pulled into the road.

They parked at the Lighthouse looking into the night.

"Does this remind you of anything?" Samantha asked.

"What?"

"This – sitting and watching the stars."

"I did it a lot as a kid."

"Me, too."

"I was told by an old teacher that I could make a wish to the brightest starts in the sky and it would be granted. All I needed to do was find the brightest star."

"What did you always wish for?"

"For a family. A loving one. And then when I got older, all I wanted was to be able to live here in Aruba."

Samantha smiled. "I guess we could say your wishes came true."

"Some of it. Some of it. What about you? What did you always wish for?"

"A sister. A younger sister, though."

"And then came Ash."

"Yeah, years later, she showed up. I never knew I had a sister before she showed up. And she affected my life in more ways than I could have known at that time."

They remained quiet now. Maybe it was because they both didn't want to talk about Ash or perhaps, they just fancied their own silence. Richard reached out and held Samantha's hand. She let him hold on to her hand.

"Do you feel as I feel, Samantha?" he asked.

Samantha remained quiet.

"Do you?"

She chose not to answer. Her chest was beating fast now. She couldn't speak. She knew she should get out of the car now or tell him to drive her home. But she just sat there, feeling her chest rise and fall, her throat tightening.

When his hips found hers, she welcomed it. She kissed him back hungrily. He kissed her neck and fondled her breasts. She gasped as he squeezed them. When his finger began creeping up her thighs, she parted her legs invitingly. Richard pushed her panties to the side and let his fingers caress her clitoris. Samantha let out a moan. Richard felt fulfilled.

He kept at it, kissing and fingering her until her body began to vibrate. She was moaning mindlessly now. He increased the working of his finger. He felt her raise her butt off the car seat, needing more of the ecstasy. When she gasped loudly and he felt warm fluid on his palm, he knew he had taken her to wonderland. He felt fulfilled again.

"Let's drive home," he told her.

He drove fast and in silence. There was nothing to talk about. He knew what they were going to do once they got to the house. She knew it, too. She knew it was crazy, but this was all she wanted. When a car drove too slowly in front of them, she heard him cuss. She cussed, too, very quietly.

Richard parked the car in front of the house. They got out and hastened into the house. Once he managed to close the door, he pushed her up against the wall and began to kiss her. She kissed him back and pushed her body up against him.

Suddenly, Richard pulled back from her. "Tell me to stop now, Samantha. Tell me to stop or I won't be able to."

To respond, Samantha drew him closer to her and kissed him. He kissed back. She wrapped her leg around his waist. Richard lifted her off the ground and carried her into the guest room. He undressed her fast. She helped him unbutton his shirt. When she pulled down his pants, his erect penis sprang out. She took it in her hand.

Richard pushed her into the bed. She laid there, her back tilted above the bed and her legs parted. Richard raised her legs, got into position, and then thrust home. Samantha gasped, her mouth making a perfect 'O.'

They made love fast and slow and the fast. They were at it until they climaxed and collapsed into each other's arm. They laid there breathing heavily; their chests rising and falling. And when he began to hear the slow, whistling sound of Samantha's breathing, he knew she had fallen asleep. He laid there awake for a long time, his arm wrapped around her naked body. He loved the feel of her breast on his body. He thought she had a great body; her firm breasts were a delight to his mind.

As he stayed up, he thought of the right feelings he really should have. Was he supposed to feel guilt? He thought about it. He didn't feel guilt. He couldn't. He couldn't possibly be happy; Ash died, but what just happened between him and her sister felt right to him. He couldn't help thinking he met and married the wrong sister. Samantha felt right to him.

# Chapter Fifteen

Samantha woke up to the snoring of Richard behind her and his arm around her. She stiffened. The event of last night replayed quickly and vividly in her mind. She had been crazy to allow that happened. And she wasn't even tipsy, so there was nothing to blame it on. She had just wanted and had gone ahead to sleep with her sister's husband. And she was only dead a month!

She wriggled out of his embrace and went into the toilet. She brushed her mouth and climbed into the shower. As the water began running, her thoughts traversed every recess of her mind. She thought of her sister that was no more; of the burden of guilt her mother was carrying for her demise; for the hurt of doing this with Richard, knowing she shouldn't have been in the house in the first place. She thought of the life she could have had with O'Brian, and of the pain of having to cut him out of her life. Her mind was heavy; a mess. She began to wail. Tears streamed down her cheek, mixing easily with the water from the shower.

The bathroom door opened and Richard entered. He went to her and pulled her into his arms. She leaned on him and cried. He let her cry. When she could manage to speak, she said, "We shouldn't have. We shouldn't have."

He said nothing.

"It's so wrong," she said.

"It feels so right. Why does it feel so right?"

He kissed her. She didn't kiss him back. But she didn't push him away. He leaned closer to her until their foreheads were against each other.

"I don't know why I didn't meet you. I wish it was you I met, Sammy."

"Don't say that," Samantha protested.

"I feel I should have been patient."

"It's such a wrong thing to say. It's wrong."

"I don't feel any guilt about us. I tried with Ash; I went into that relationship promising to do my best. In the end, it didn't work out."

Samantha just leaned against him.

"I feel right with you, Sammy."

He kissed her and she gave in. Their bodies were pressed together and the warmth was spreading. They made love again. This time, it was slow and tender. It felt sweet in a different way from last night. Samantha found herself losing her senses and emotions to him. She climaxed suppressing herself from screaming his name.

After they had made love, Samantha left the bathroom and went into the room. Richard continued to shower. His thought stayed with her. He was in love with her, he thought.

In the room, Samantha flopped into bed. She curled into a fetal position and closed her eyes. She felt her eyes hurt from closing it too tightly. She opened it and seeing her sister's coat on the bed, she pulled it close to herself. If Ash walked into this room now, it'd feel like she had come around and gotten her vengeance. But it was never that. She didn't know what it was.

She felt something hard in the coat and raised it up to see. She couldn't see it. But she continued to feel the hard object. Further investigation showed the hard object had been sewn into the garment. She sat up in bed, frowning. She began to search for scissor.

Richard hurried into the room with a towel around his waist. He had rushed with his shower, fearing Samantha might be gone before he returned to the room. He didn't want her out of his sight. It was time to know her more and let her know him. He was pleased to see she was still in the room. He frowned, however, when he saw she was cutting away fabrics of the coat he gave her with a scissors.

"What are you doing?" he asked her.

Samantha finished up and extricated a small jotter from the cloth. Richard was surprised.

"What is it?" he asked.

Samantha opened the jotter and flipped through. It seemed to be a book holding the data of the men Ash was having affairs with. The more they studied the book, the more they concluded it was. It had phone numbers and initials of names, dates of meeting and the places. Some of the initials appeared twice.

Richard was stunned. It wasn't like he hadn't known of Ash's indiscretion, but he hadn't known it ran this deep. It was paralyzing. Samantha looked up at him and saw how affected he was by this. She placed her hand over his.

"I'm sorry about this," she said.

"For what? You don't have to. Ash chose her life and you shouldn't apologize on her behalf."

"Still…"

"It's fine."

Indeed, Richard was fine. It further justified his feelings for Samantha and wiped away any modicum of regret that may settle in his mind. Maybe, after all, Ash was the architect of her own death.

Samantha traced the initials with her hand.

"One of these men got Ash pregnant," she said, "and the one who got her pregnant would likely lead us closer to the truth."

"You have a good point. It may mean that he had a higher motive to do it."

Richard began walking out of the room. "You have to get dressed. Let's go for breakfast."

"And this book, what do we do with it?"

"I will go through it at the restaurant to see what I can find. Afterwards, I call the police to submit it. They could easily trace the phone numbers and from there, locate the man Ash spent her last day with."

"All right."

Richard left the room. She got up and got dressed. Her sister stayed on her mind as she did. Was Ash losing her mind in her last days on earth? It was ridiculous that a woman could keep such a number of sex partners. It was insane.

When Richard called her, she was ready. She picked up the jotter and left the room.

The restaurant was quiet with only a handful of people there when they entered. Richard ordered coffee, while they waited for their sandwiches and orange juice. They were silent. Richard was busy making a replica of the jotter in another note and looking through the initials carefully to see it any of them was familiar.

Samantha watched him work. She thought about what their lives were evolving into and wondered if it was so because they were both emotionally shaken. Perhaps, once this whole tragedy blew off, they'd find out they didn't belong together and moved on. For now, she was certain she was feeling this man. When he sat up abruptly and cross-checked a number on the jotter on his phone, Samantha wondered what he had found out. His face was focused and furrowed. He stood up.

"What is it?" Samantha asked.

"I have to go."

"Why? What is it?"

"Something I must do. Here, take this jotter to the police. Tell them it was discovered from Ash's things and that it may prove useful."

"Okay. But where—"

Richard walked over and kissed her lightly. Then he walked away.

As Richard drove his car, he wished all the slow-moving vehicles on the way would disappear. He had little patience. It was Saturday morning, so he couldn't understand why the roads were even busy. He pulled into Eric's compound and went to pound on the door.

Eric opened the door to find an enraged Richard standing there. He was shocked. But it was the debilitating punch from Richard that shocked him more. He reeled over and fell. He held his face. His upper lip was broken and blood found its way out.

"What the hell, Richard?"

"You don't ask me what the hell. I ask you what the hell! What the hell where you doing sleeping around with my wife? You thought I'll never find out? And you were my friend. Eric, you were my friend!" Richard was like a raging bull.

"Now you have to calm the hell down, Richard."

"You don't tell me what to do, you bastard! You're a bastard! Screwing my wife like…"

"You don't get to blame me, Richard. Blame your wife for coming at me. And blame yourself for whatever you did to her emotions…"

"You say those words to me, Eric? You do such atrocious thing and you think you hold a moral standing to point fingers."

"Don't blame me for you issues!"

"You son of a bitch! Fuck you!"

He looked up to see that Margaret was standing behind her husband, staring coldly as they exchanged word. It dawned on him that she wasn't even shocked to hear her husband slept with Ash. It was a bitter awakening for him. He turned to Eric.

"Did you kill her, too?"

"How could you ask me that?"

"Did you?" Richard shouted.

"No. I could never do such a thing."

Richard chuckled.

"You could never, huh? I could have sworn that you could never sleep with my wife; that you were my closest friend. I could have sworn you were a good man…" He chuckled. "Now, I don't know what to believe anymore."

"Eric can never put a finger on another. He definitely didn't kill Ash," Margaret said.

Richard looked up at her. He was deeply saddened by their conspiracy and shared secret against him. "You knew he was screwing Ash and you said nothing."

Margaret didn't look away. She stared at him coldly.

"Why are you even with him?" Richard asked. "Why?"

"He apologized and that's what matters," said Margaret. "I forgave him and we are moving on."

Richard spat on the floor. He was disgusted by the two of them. To think they were the people closest to him; the ones he had shared all his woes with. It weakened him.

"Anyway, if you must know," he said, "Ash made a list of the men she was with. Your name and number is there, Eric. The list is now with the police. They will be calling on you to explain your role in her death. Be ready."

He left the house. He was, finally, heart-broken.

# Chapter Sixteen

Detective Andrew and his smiling face were on seat to receive Samantha and her little book.

"What do we have here?" he asked.

Samantha sat across from him and watched him flip through the pages.

"A list," she said. "I believe it's a list of names of the men Ash was involved with…" She shrugged. "Sexually."

"Numbers and initials and dates."

Samantha nodded.

"This is impressive. It is the closest we have come to interviewing any other suspect beside her husband. We will get to work."

"That's good. Any other thing I need to know?"

"Em… no!"

"And O'Brian?"

"Oh, O'Brian. He has not been cooperative. He insists he can only talk in the presence of his lawyer. And now, the law and crime specialists are handling that. I should have feedback for you in a day or two."

"That's fine." Samantha couldn't help but think the case was more complicated than she had thought. "In the absence of any further business, may I take my leave, officer?"

"Naturally, you may, but…" He smiled. "There is just one more business."

"That would be?"

"I would love it if you would have dinner with me."

"Oh!" Samantha thought about it. The detective didn't particular look like her type. He appeared a tad uncouth. But she felt she needed something different. She had been around Richard long now and all these feelings for him had been building in her. Perhaps, it would be different if she spent more time with someone else.

"All right, when?" she asked.

"Tonight is great."

"Okay."

"You may need to give me your number."

Samantha gave him her number. "How about you give me yours?"

"Oh. Okay."

Samantha took down his number and his name. "I will call you."

She left. The detective smiled to himself. He felt fulfilled.

Samantha walked slowly along Boardwalk. She thought of what to occupy her time with and settled on shopping. Some of those outfits she saw at the plaza were great. She reckoned she could buy a couple, especially, as she hadn't brought enough clothes with her.

She went into the plaza. The dresses she saw some days back had been sold. But there were other amazing ones. Samantha didn't like shopping that much; she believed she spent more than she needed to whenever she went to the stores. She reminded herself she was running low on finance and needed only two dresses.

It was while shopping that the pictures began to fit together. The detective's name was Andy Andrew. There had been such initials 'A. A.' in the list. Somehow, she was convinced he was the one. He had stared at her shocked the first time she met him and she had had to ask him if he knew her sister well. She needed to be sure of his number.

Now that she was suspicious of the detective, she wasn't sure how best to deal with the situation. She had concluded she was not going to mention her date to Richard, but she wasn't sure anymore. She needed to meet Andrew to find out what he knew and whatever role he played. She didn't think he killed Ash, but she was not going to vouch for anyone. She was certain Richard might talk her out of meeting with the detective, for whatever reason he may come up with. She thought, now, it was best she kept the information away from him. She would meet the detective on her own terms.

When Samantha got home, Richard was not there. She went to lie down on the bed and before long, she was napping. When she woke up, Richard still wasn't home. It would be much later in the evening that he returned. She heard him slam the door shut and immediately went down the stairs to meet him. They met at the foot of the stairs and Richard embraced and kissed her.

"Are you all right?" she asked him.

"I am just tired." He pulled away from her. "Would you betray me, too?"

"What do you mean?"

"I'm just tired. In as much as I knew of Ash's cheating, it was pretty distressing knowing they were so many. And to realize a friend of mine, my best friends, actually, was one of them…"

"Oh my god!" Samantha was horrified.

Richard laughed sadly. "And his wife knew. I would go to these people's house and pour my heart out and they were screwing my wife!"

"I'm so sorry."

"It broke my heart. It depresses me more than Ash's cheating. I feel foolish. I don't know who to trust anymore."

Samantha knew she couldn't hold back anything concerning Ash from him any longer. He was suffering and she didn't want to be a part of it.

"I found something," she said.

"What?"

"First, I will be going on a date tonight with Detective Andrew…"

"Why would you want to do that?"

Samantha sensed jealousy in Richard's voice. "The other thing is that his initials 'A. A.' matched one of those on the list."

"Really? Oh!"

"Let's check it against the number he gave me. You still have your copy, right? We will know if he is the one."

They went upstairs to the guest room. Richard brought out the note from his back pocket. He found the initials. Samantha called the detective's number from her phone and it matched the one on Richard's note.

"Is there someone she didn't screw?" Richard said bitterly.

"Interestingly, he appeared only once in her list," Samantha noted, "and it was only three days before her death. What were they up to?"

"If Ash had been alive, maybe there might have been other times."

"I don't know," Samantha said, "I could almost sense that she went to him because she might be in trouble and he began making passes. Ash gave in."

Richard looked at her with raised brows.

"He is making passes at me, too. So, I figure he likes making passes at women."

"The bastard!" Richard cussed.

"So what now?"

"He could be dangerous. We have to be careful with him."

"I want to go on that date with him," Samantha said resolutely.

Richard frowned. "You don't have to. Ash is dead, shot six times, and now you want to go on a date with an armed man who also went on a date with your deceased sister."

"I have to find out what he knows."

"I forbid you! You won't go on that date!"

Samantha looked at him. She understood he was trying to protect her, but she felt he was overdoing it. Maybe his feelings for her were getting the better of him.

"Richard," she began patiently, "if this man had a hand in my sister's death, I intend to find that out. And I need to know why. Isn't this why I came here? Unless you have a better plan, I think I should go on that date with him."

"I have no better plan, but this is just... just dangerous."

"We will be in a restaurant. I am not going anywhere else with him."

"I will go with you."

She looked at him. "Come on!"

"I won't sit there with both of you, Sammy. I will just be somewhere in the background. To make sure everything is all right."

"That's fine." She pulled him close and kissed him. "I have to go get ready."

"In that case, allow me to help you shower."

"Oh, it's like that now?"

"It is." He laughed and kissed her.

# Chapter Seventeen

It was a busy restaurant. Samantha thought it was a tad too noisy. Richard wouldn't have brought her here. She understood the detective earned way less that the insurance guru and the difference was showing. The detective tried to make everything sound funny and Samantha thought she was trying too hard. She laughed dutifully to his jokes and wondered how long she'd keep up with that. The man repulsed her and she wondered if her sister felt any differently.

As they waited for their order to arrive, Samantha wondered where Richard was. She couldn't make him out from the people around and she didn't want to try to find him. The man was a detective and would know if she tried to search Richard out. It was good he had no impression of her.

Richard watched them talk and laugh. She was a little upset that Samantha was enjoying the man's company. He wondered if she was even minding the business of the night and finding what she needed to find out. When he reached out and touched her arm and Samantha seemed to yield, he hated it.

He watched Detective Andrew talk and move. There was something off, something malicious, about him. He didn't like it. He looked dangerous, like his laughter was mere screenshot of deceit. He wished he never agreed to this and now he was worried for her. When a man and his lover stood in front of him kissing, he wanted to shove them both to the ground. He patiently waited for them to move on, as he didn't want to attract attention to himself.

Richard wished he had placed a mic on Samantha. That way he'd hear every word they were saying and perhaps, be calmer. When Samantha got up, he wondered why she was getting up. He followed her with his eyes and understood she was going to the restroom. He got up to follow her. He took one last look at the detective and saw him rummaging his pants' pocket. He thought something was about to happen here. He quickly brought out his phone and video-recorded the detective discreetly drop something into Samantha's glass. He hurried away, then, to Samantha.

He waited outside the restroom until Samantha came out. He hugged her and Samantha wondered if he just missed her or relieved to see that she was all right. He pulled her to one side.

"What's going on?" he asked her.

"Nothing much. He insists he doesn't know Ash and had never met her."

"He denied? Why then did he slip something into your drink?"

Samantha gasped. "He did? My God!"

"Okay, I need you to not take a sip of that drink."

"Okay."

Richard planted his lips on hers. "I need to keep you alive. I need nothing to happen to you... so I can court you properly. So I can talk to you, so I can convince you not to leave Aruba."

Samantha didn't know what to say. Richard kissed her hard and told her to go. "Just go, I will call the police."

She left. Richard's eyes followed her all the way. Then he placed the call to inform them of what was happening.

He went back to his position and resumed watching them. He saw the detective talking and gesturing toward the glass of drink. He knew he was persuading her to take the drink. Samantha refused. He saw the slight anger on the man's face. He saw him try to persuade her some more. It was not working. The man became quiet and unsmiling. Richard feared what he might do next. He was relieved to find two policemen making their way to the table where Samantha sat.

They were trying to arrest him when he got enraged. Richard began running toward the table. At the same time, the detective was grabbing at Samantha.

"You bitch! You set me up!" he howled.

The entire restaurant was disturbed. Richard got to the table and slipped his arm around Samantha's waist to calm her.

"I was the one who called you," he said to the police. "This man is a suspect for killing my wife."

Detective Andrew was enraged. The policemen tried to restrain him. "You mean that Ash bitch? I didn't kill that bitch! But I damn well hoped I did. I wanted to. She is nothing but trash, the lowest of bitches. She'd rather blow a cop than get arrested for DUI."

The policemen arrested him and took him out. The detective kept on spewing expletives. Richard hugged Samantha and tried to keep her from crying.

On the way back to the house, Richard turned to Samantha who was yet to say a word. "I am happy it's all over now. We can start worrying."

Samantha frowned. "All over? He didn't say he did it."

"Oh, come on, Samantha, you don't think he'd say he did it."

"Well, even if he did, we still don't know why."

Richard exhaled tiredly. She was right. They were not done with this yet.

When they got home, Richard led her to the guest-room and asked if she needed anything. She needed nothing.

"All right then, have a good night."

Samantha showered and retired in bed. She thought of the detective. He looked like he was capable of killing Ash. He was uncouth and aggressive and armed. She wondered what business he had with Ash and hoped the police would investigate him quickly. It was a long time before she slept. When she did, it was marred by nightmares. She wished Richard had come to sleep in her room.

# Chapter Eighteen

Samantha was at the beach, wearing a loose-fitting shirt and short. She was sitting in a lean-in chair reading a book. It had been three days since Detective Andrew got arrested, but there was no word still from the police. She was called into the precinct the next day to give an account of what went down at the restaurant and after that, nothing. She felt maybe she was in a haste for news or she just wanted some progress.

She thought about it. Progress. She wanted progress. Things had stalled with Richard. At the restaurant, perhaps overwhelmed by the emotions surrounding the danger she was in, he had stated they needed to talk. He had insinuated that he wanted her not to leave Aruba, but he hadn't mentioned it again. Samantha was worried, wondering if he was emotionally confused or something. They needed to have that discussion, so she could define her hold on life.

When she came to the beach to read, she had intended to do just that – read. But she hadn't read two chapters all day. Her mind had been occupied with thoughts of Richard. Sometimes, she thought he was suffering, having seen his world turned upside down. When he smiled at her, he saw sadness in his eyes. He hadn't been in her room to sleep, she was fine with it, but she wished she knew what was going on with him.

Her phone rang, startling her. It was her mother on the phone. She sighed. How much she had forgotten to keep in touch with that woman. She took the call.

"Hello, Mum?"

"Sammy, dear, how are you?"

Samantha thought her mother sounded good. She was happy she didn't need to manage the situation. "I am well, Mum. How are you?"

"I'm good. That boy of yours came again."

Samantha gasped. Then she smiled. "Oh, Peter."

"He's a nice man."

Samantha had to change the subject. She knew what her mother would say next. "The police have made some headway," she said.

"Oh that's good. Tell me."

"It was a policeman. He had seen Ash a few days before her death. I think they were dating. So, the police have him in custody. He confessed to having the intention of killing her."

"Oh!"

"Yes, Mum. I will wait a few more days for the outcome of the investigation and then I will call you about returning home."

"That's all right, my dear. How about Ash's husband? You have a perception of him now?"

"Yes, Mum."

"Tell me."

"I think he is a good guy. I think Ash really didn't treat him right." She sighed. "She cheated on him and she didn't do it with just one man."

"Oh, Ash."

Samantha wanted to tell her Ash was pregnant with another man before she got killed, but she didn't. It might break her mother's heart.

"I hope she finds the peace in death, that this life couldn't offer her," Rose said.

"I hope so, too."

"Sammy, dear, have you been eating?"

"Yes, Mum."

"That's good. When you call that young man, Peter, tell him I'm grateful."

"I will, Mum."

"Goodbye, dear."

"Bye, Mum."

Samantha couldn't tell why, but this phone call with her mother made her feel good. Maybe it was because of the different disposition the woman had and the fact that she didn't need to manage her emotionally. She knew she would have to leave here. There was nothing for her anymore; the police had a list to work with and had made an arrest, she was no longer needed. It hurt her as she thought about it. She would have to leave Aruba and Richard.

A shadow fell on her body. She looked up and saw it was Richard. She felt joy inside. She was smiling up at him when she saw he looked sober and crestfallen.

"What's wrong, Richard?"

Richard simply dropped languidly on the sand next to her. He was still in his work clothes. Samantha sat up, alarmed.

"Richard, what is it?"

"I just got a call. Eric is dead."

"Eric?"

"My friend, the one who slept with Ash."

"Oh no!" Samantha didn't exactly know what to feel, but sympathy didn't come close. She didn't think Eric was a nice guy, so she was surprised that his death affected Richard the way it did. "I'm sorry to hear that," she said, hoping to please him.

"There is just a lot happening," Richard said. "Too many things. And all at once."

Samantha could feel he was stressed. She brought his head close and put it on her laps.

"I am beginning to rethink life. Like, is it even worth it to struggle to work so hard?"

"Richard, just relax. Allow me touch your back. You will be fine."

She rubbed his back slowly, deliberately, with her palm, and then with the tip of her fingers, varying the pressure, so that Richard was made consistently aware of her touch. He found himself relaxing, thinking only of her touch, and how it pleased his body. She even began to hum a song. Richard couldn't place the tune, but it was soft and appropriate. He thought about it, *This is what a mother would do for a child.*

He chuckled quietly.

And then, like a rude shock, he was thrown off balance mentally. His mind forced an image on him. It was a memory he had suppressed over the years. It came playing in vivid colors and he found himself shaking.

Audrey was sitting opposite him at the back of the classroom. They were sharing Audrey's lunch. Audrey was the kid who had everything. They said his parents were rich; richer than the parents of all the other kids in the classroom combined. Even at age thirteen, Richard knew it was a lie. But there was no denying that Audrey's folks were wealthy. Audrey wore the best shoes and jackets and went to the priciest of places for holidays with his parents. Audrey was their only child.

Audrey's birthday party, three weeks ago, had been the talk for an entire week. There were two celebrations; one in school and the other in Audrey's home. The kids had gorged themselves with food. They had even returned to their homes with gifts from Audrey's parents.

The day Audrey told Richard that he'd love Richard to be at his birthday party, Richard had simply asked him who else was coming. Audrey immediately knew why he asked the question. Richard couldn't be in the company of some of their classmates. They were bullies who, at every turn, reminded Richard that he didn't have real parents, because he was evil and killed his parents at birth, and that he wore torn clothes and looked horrible. Audrey had simply told Richard that he was inviting him first and together, they would invite only the kids Richard was cool with.

Richard had been moved by this. He asked Audrey, "Why did you choose to be my friend? Why do you want to do what I want?"

Richard was not used to someone wanting to be his friend that much.

Audrey had only moved to that school a year ago. He said to Richard, "Last year, I didn't have parents, too. I still wouldn't have had one if my parents didn't come to adopt me."

Richard gasped. He wouldn't have thought Audrey was adopted.

"So, when I came to this school and heard you didn't have parents," Audrey said, "I thought to myself, *We are alike*, and that's why I want to be your friend."

Richard had been moved by this. Audrey told him he had been bullied before in his former school and had been called horrible names and that he totally understood what Richard was going through.

Audrey would bring a huge portion of meal to school and let Richard share with him. He became the best-friend Richard never had. Richard began to go to Audrey's house after school. But he always made sure he returned to the state-provided home before 5:30 p.m.

One evening, Audrey and Richard had gone to the bakery to get bread. Audrey's mother wanted to make toast bread, but found out she had run out of bread. Audrey and Richard volunteered to run down to the bakery to get some. Audrey never made it back home. He got knocked down by a car. The driver never even stopped to see if the boy's life could be saved.

For weeks, Richard was mournful. He understood at that age what loss meant. He loved Audrey. He was hurt that he had to die. He had so many questions.

When Richard grew older, he learnt to shoo away thoughts of Audrey. The thoughts left him depressed for days. Richard learnt to suppress it. But here, with Eric gone, the thoughts of Audrey re-surfaced.

Samantha noticed he was shaking. She made him sit up.

"What's wrong?" she asked him, alarmed.

"I am fine," Richard said.

"Fine my ass! You don't look close to it."

She took on of his hands in hers. Then she checked his eyes' color.

"What? You're going to doctor me now?" Richard asked weakly.

"Do you need a doctor?"

"I will be fine." Richard tried to sound brave.

"I didn't know Eric's death would affect you this much."

"He was my best-friend. I did love and accept him once. And that has not been too long ago."

"I remember losing a friend, too," Samantha said. "She was the closest I had to a sister. I was ten."

"She died?"

"No," Samantha said, "she left. She didn't even tell me she was leaving. She just left."

"Maybe she didn't have the chance to say goodbye."

Samantha sighed. "That's what hurt me the most then. She did have the chance to say goodbye, but she chose not to. I was hurt to find out that a lot of kids, back then, knew she was leaving, yet she never told me. It was too much betrayal for me. I suffered for a long time."

Richard thought of Audrey. His death had done that for him, too. They had had plans about places to go and things to do and he had just abandoned them all and left.

136

Samantha cuddled him now. "Let's put this demon away. We will go to Eric's house right away."

Richard was going to visit Margaret anyway. Only, he was now glad that Samantha was coming as well. She helped him up and they began to make their way back to the house.

# Chapter Nineteen

Samantha thought the black dress she wore to her sister's graveside would be fitting to wear to Margaret's. She thought so because Eric's death was important to Richard. She wondered how best to handle him after going to see Margaret. Her mother aside, she hadn't been in that place where she had to manage the emotions of a love-interest. She hoped Richard would deal with the situation well. She admitted Richard felt better after they returned to the house from the beach and she made him drink coffee.

She had also made him go into his room to shower and get ready. She didn't want him using the bathroom in the guest room, just in case he needed to cry a little. She didn't want her presence to prevent him from doing so.

She was struggling to zip the dress when Richard knocked, opened the door, and walked in. She turned and looked at him. He looked sharp in his white shirt. His black suit hung on his shoulder. Samantha smiled at him lightly.

Richard angled toward her as she stood in front of the mirror. He touched the zip, so she relaxed to let him help her with it. But what Richard did shock her. In swift movements, he pulled the dress up and squeezed her butts. Then he ran his hands over her thighs and pressed his groin at her. She felt him get hard right away. He pulled her panties down. His movement, the intention, his need, fired Samantha up. She needed him, too.

Richard unbuckled his belt hastily. In seconds, his trouser went flying on the floor. He pulled Samantha into position. Samantha bent her back and pushed herself back, providing Richard the right level and angel to use to his advantage. Richard pushed into her hungrily.

Samantha felt him go into her. She was eclipsed with sensation. They pushed hard against each other, making the best of each thrust. Richard moaned into her ears. Samantha kept her eyes open, watching both of their faces etched with the pleasures that engulfed them. She moaned. The entirety of her wanted him to keep going. She encouraged him with her moans. "Go, baby! Yeah! Ouh… yes baby!"

By the time they were both spent, Richard reeled backward and collapsed into the bed. Samantha joined him, collapsing on top of him.

"I should have thought about that," Samantha said. "That's what we both needed."

Richard waited to catch his breath. Lines of sweat had formed on his forehead. His chest rose and fell.

"That was something," he said.

"Came out of nowhere," Samantha said. "You should have said all the while that this was the therapy you needed. I am not stingy."

Richard laughed. "I had no plan of doing this. I just saw you looking that way and it couldn't have gone any other way."

Samantha laughed. Richard cuddled her in his arm. "You are beautiful," he told her.

Samantha was pleased to know that he found her beautiful.

"Stay with me," he said to her.

Samantha wanted to pretend she had no idea what he was talking about, but she knew this was a moment of sincerity for him and it was important she didn't kid with it.

"It's too soon," she said.

"I know. I have been thinking about it… waiting to feel unsure of what I want. But each day, I am convinced the more that I want to be with you."

"It's too soon," Samantha repeated.

"All right," Richard said, "stay until the summer holidays end. I hope things will be clearer for the two of us then. I admit we both need more time to know each other."

"That's fine." Samantha was now thinking about the best thing to tell her mother if she asked why she hadn't returned still. Surely, she was not going to tell her she was screwing Ash's husband now. She felt a stab of guilt. As if Richard could read her thoughts, he held her closer.

"We do have a visit to pay," Samantha said teasingly.

"Oh that, I almost forgot." Richard chuckled. He released her and got up. Samantha watched his hard butts as he dashed into the bathroom. He cleaned himself up and got out. "Go get ready, Sammy."

"I just want to sleep. I'm tired."

Richard began dragging her out of the bed. Samantha giggled.

Samantha noticed Richard was smiling a lot now as they got into the car. She wondered if it was the sex they just had or the fact that she had agreed to stay with him for the remainder of the summer. He was chatty all the way to

Margaret's place and Samantha was relieved she didn't have to deal with his somberness.

Margaret opened the door to let them in. Richard thought she looked whitish. He felt so sorry for her. "Come in," she said.

Samantha followed after Richard. She noticed Margaret's face on seeing her. As she walked into the living room and took a seat next to Richard, she felt the woman's gaze on her. It was troubling. Samantha thought she was losing color.

"I am so, so sorry about this loss," Richard said. "You do not deserve this Margaret. I am sorry."

"Ms. Marshall, do accept my condolence," Samantha chipped in. She was not comfortable with the way Margaret stared at her, like she was horrified to see her. "Is something wrong, Ms. Marshall?"

"You just look so much alike – you and her."

Samantha nodded her understanding.

"Were you two close?"

"Unfortunately, no."

"How did he die?" Richard asked.

Margaret didn't even hear him. "I can understand why the two of you were never close. Ash was such a bitch!"

Richard and Samantha were shocked to hear this. They looked at one another and then turned to Margaret. None of them knew the best way to react.

Margaret turned to Richard. "Are you a sucker for relationship drama, eh? Are you like a glutton who feeds on heartbreaks and being cheated on?"

Richard was too caught by surprise to think straight. His jaw had dropped a few millimeters.

"She cheated on you for so long. She was nothing but a parasite. Yet, you tolerated her. Who does that? And here, now, you've decided to tag along another Ash."

Samantha didn't expect any of the things she was hearing and she knew it couldn't be down to her losing her husband alone. When she found the voice to speak, she said, "I am Samantha, not Ash."

Margaret laughed. It was eerie and distant. "Of course, I know that. I already did away with the other bitch!"

"What?" Samantha exclaimed.

Richard's jaw dropped now to the lowest it possibly could.

Margaret laughed some more and went to pour herself a large drink. She gulped down half of it and grimaced. Then she returned to stand some distance away from the duo.

"Ash began fucking my husband when I traveled for a doctor's appointment in New Jersey. I heard he was the best gynecologist out there. By the time I returned, she was already fucking him. I didn't see them on my bed, but I knew. Eric changed the sheet and had it washed, but he couldn't wash away the woman's smell from our room. Richard, you would know of her heavy perfume. That woman emptied a bottle on herself each day. So, she was fucking my husband!" She laughed again and sipped from her glass. She was beginning to look drunk.

"On my return, I knew. I said nothing to Eric. And then, he began meeting with her in the hotel. It was utterly disgusting. I was aghast. How could the wife of my husband's best-friend lure him away from me? I was confused. Do I talk to Eric about it? What if he was in love

142

with her and decided to leave me? Do I talk to the bitch about it? What if she laughed in my face? See how I suffered?" She sipped from her glass. "And then she got pregnant…"

Richard stood up and sat back down in his seat. Samantha could tell he was mesmerized by these revelations. She was, too. *So, it was Eric that Ash got pregnant with.*

"I found out she was pregnant. It was easy. They got careless. They began to use a particular hotel room…" She chuckled. "I got one of the attendants there to work for me – for a little token naturally. I placed a small camera in the room. I got the info I needed."

She chuckled again. "Funny, I paid the attendant with Eric's money."

She sipped from her glass again. There was only small liquor left in the cup now. "I confronted Eric then," she said. "I asked him to make his choice. The options were to apologize to me and pay me whatever compensation I wanted or face a divorce from me, in addition to having the video I made released to you. Of course, he chose the first option. And that came with a clause." She chuckled and finished her drink. "The clause was to get Ash to terminate the baby."

Samantha and Richard sat there looking at her. They watched her go back to fill her cup. This time, she just carried the cup back to where she stood without taking a sip.

"Eric, poor, naïve Eric, he didn't know how to get that bitch to remove the baby. He even termed it *his baby*. What a pity? He couldn't even see that the pregnancy was going to be a milk factory for that bitch. She was going to milk him for life. He didn't know what to do. I volunteered to help him get Ash to terminate the baby. He agreed. He cajoled Ash to come to the house, told her I was away. Eric wasn't even home. He was at work. He thought I was going to talk to Ash. He thought I had a magic wand to get her to terminate the pregnancy. When he returned home, he found Ash's dead body in the garage, shot six times."

"Oh no!" Samantha felt a throaty scream escape her. The tears came rolling down her cheek.

Margaret was aloof. She sipped from her glass cup. She was not looking at any of them. She didn't care about them.

Richard struggled to find composure. "Did Eric know about this – that you killed Ash?"

"He knew, silly," Margaret said simply. "I already said he returned home to find her dead body in his garage. He was alarmed at first. He shook like a baby and when some sense returned to him, he helped me move her body."

"Eric helped you move her body?" Richard asked disbelievingly.

"To the beach, yes. I suggested we tie a metal to her leg and dump her in the ocean, but Eric said the beach was fine enough. I know a part of him wanted her to be found, so she could at least have a decent burial. Does that shit even matter? The bitch was going to burn in hell anyway and did not in any way deserve a decent burial."

"You witch!" Samantha roared. She rose and reached out to grab Margaret. Richard held her back. Samantha screamed.

"You witch!" she cried and struggled with Richard.

Margaret finished her drink and walked briskly to a cupboard. When Samantha and Richard were able to look up, they found Margaret holding a pistol in her right hand. Richard quickly pushed Samantha behind him.

Samantha was scared. Her heart raced. She shook behind Richard. She didn't want to die now; not this way, not this place.

"Margaret, please," Richard pleaded, "drop the gun."

Margaret merely chuckled.

"Drop the gun, please. It doesn't have to be this way…"

"Now you asked how he died. It was simple; I simply pushed him down the stairs. I realized we were no longer living; we were just existing. I realized I didn't love him anymore and he was the architect of that. This morning, he pushed me again. He told me he should have chosen the option of divorce and that Ash would have still been alive. He said he lost you, Richard, as a friend, despite not divorcing me, because he didn't want you to know of his affair with your wife. How dare he say those things to me? He blamed me for his excesses. He was crazy."

She waved the gun about now. Richard cringed. But Margaret wasn't even looking at him and Samantha.

"So, when he dressed up to leave for work, after telling me to start considering divorce with him, I knew I was done with him. I simply crept up behind him and pushed him down the stairs." Tears crept down her eyes now. "I guess you can't keep what is meant to be lost. I chose my options and now I am damaged."

She waved the gun again.

"Put it away, please, Marg, we have done nothing wrong," Richard said.

"Fool!" Margaret hissed. "The bullet isn't for you. It is for me!"

She pointed the gun to her head, laughed, and pulled the trigger. Samantha screamed and held tightly onto Richard. Hours later, she would still be sobbing. She was inconsolable. Richard held her tightly all through it. He wished he didn't bring her here. He ushered her outside and fished for his phone. As he dialed 911, he realized his fingers were shaking.

"There has been an emergency," he stammered into the phone and gave the address.

It took the police fifteen minutes to pull-up. They found Richard and Samantha outside. Richard answered the immediate questions they had and excused himself, "I need to take her home. I will be at your office in the morning for further clarifications."

They drove in silence. Samantha had stopped sobbing now, but her eyes were swollen and she appeared jaded. Richard's thought was occupied with Margaret's final moments; how she had laughed and appeared to accept her death with pleasure. He thought she was totally psychotic. It was paralyzing. Margaret was the most cool-headed person he ever knew. But at that point, she looked like something straight out of a thriller movie.

Richard pulled into the compound and killed the engine. Samantha sat docile in her seat. Richard helped her out of the car and into the house. He put her to bed. They lay side by side. None of them slept. They just lay there, victims of their own thoughts.

While Samantha mourned her sister afresh, Richard nursed a broken-heart. It was hurtful to learn, now, that his friend Eric knew about his wife's death in so much detail that he became an accomplice, yet pretended to be helpful to him all along. He felt so tired. He knew he would have to be careful with whom he called friend. Apparently, the title was a tad exaggerating.

The police called on Richard in the morning and he and Samantha were able to narrate the event better for them. When they left, Samantha said, "My god, so that wasn't a dream!"

Richard gave her coffee to drink and suggested they ate out. "Let's have distractions," he said.

Samantha thought her visit to Aruba had been exhilarating. It had everything she wasn't equipped for. Tragedy. Surprises. Chaos. Craze. Sex. They were too many. She wished the coming week would go so smoothly. But it didn't.

The morning after, Richard resumed running again. He told himself he had dealt enough with his emotions and it was time to get back to physical excellence. That morning, alone in the house, Samantha called her mother.

"Ash's killer is dead," she said to her once she took the call. She heard her mother gasp.

"He is dead? How? Has there been a judgment already?"

"There is no need for judgment. She shot herself already."

"Wait! What? She?"

"Yes, a woman is responsible for her death." Samantha heard her gasp again. "She is the wife of one of the men Ash was cheating with."

"So, she killed Ash?"

"She did. She found out Ash was pregnant with her husband's child…"

"Ash was pregnant?"

Samantha bit her lips. She had avoided telling her mother that all this while; she didn't want the woman any more broken than she had been in the past.

"She was. This woman found out and then she killed Ash. She shot Ash, Mother."

"Dear Lord!"

"She got her husband to help her dispose of Ash's body and then she killed him. Later, she killed herself, too."

Rose sobbed now. "She is mean, wicked, no-good woman."

"It's over now, Mum."

Rose waited a few seconds before speaking, "Are you coming home?"

"Not immediately, Mum."

"Oh. I'd have thought—"

"I know, Mum. But I've seen too much here to just return home. I need purging, Mum. I will stick it out here throughout summer."

"Are you all right where you are, baby?"

"I'm fine."

"You're eating well?"

"I am, Mum."

"Great. Could you do one thing for me?"

"What, Mum?"

"Could you go to Ash's grave to tell her that I'm sorry?"

Samantha frowned. "Mum, she's dead and won't hear that. Moreover, it was not your fault—"

"Sammy! Could you do that for me?"

Samantha stopped talking. "All right, Mum."

"Good."

They talked a little more before Samantha hung up. She wasn't convinced her mother took the entire news well. She dialed Peter's number. "Hello, Peter."

"Samantha, hello. How is Aruba treating you?"

"It's crazy. I will be here a little longer."

"In that case, I might have to check on your mother on your behalf."

"Exactly. I was just calling to... Oh, Peter, I am grateful."

"Rose is a great woman. I enjoy her company. It's certainly easier talking to her than you."

Samantha chuckled. "Peter, she is old. She has no fancies and expectations. And with her, you don't have any. So, that's why."

Peter was quiet.

"Peter?"

"Yeah?"

"Thank you."

"You're welcome."

Later in the day, Samantha set out to the grave-yard alone. It was not easy finding Ash's grave. She had, somehow, missed the path Richard took on the day he brought her. When she found it, she noticed a woman was just leaving the grave. She had dropped a red flower, Samantha frowned. She didn't know Ash had people who cared about her. She ran toward the woman.

"Hello? Hold up!"

She saw the woman freak-out when she saw her. Samantha pretended not to notice. But the woman appeared visibly shaken. "I am her sister," she explained. "Did you know her?"

"Rose? Yes."

Samantha frowned. "Rose? Her name was Ash."

"No, it was Rose. She gave herself Ash much later. She said there was nothing Rose-like about her; that Ash suited her better."

Samantha looked back at the grave and wondered if she knew anything about her sister. Ash Blackwell. Richard had the name changed. He hadn't even mentioned it. "You knew her well then."

The woman had a small figure. Samantha thought she was in her early fifties. She had a pointed mouth that looked fitting for humorous jokes and a nose that was so small Samantha wondered how she didn't suffocate.

"I knew her parents," the woman said. "They lived in Mexico."

Samantha was surprised. This was the closest she had come to knowing Ash. "Oh really?" she asked. But the woman appeared impatient, looking back, like she was awaited.

"Can I have your number?" Samantha asked. "I will sure like to know more about her."

The woman hesitated. "Let me have yours instead."

Samantha quickly gave her number. "Please call, I'm dying to know."

The woman nodded and left. Samantha watched her leave. She walked with a limp. Samantha wondered what her story was.

She went to Ash's grave. She closed her eyes and bowed her head. "Rose, Mum is so sorry for giving you away. She regrets it. And she pleads your forgiveness."

She stood there for a long time. Then she opened her eyes. Tears rolled down her cheek. This was going to be her last visit.

# Chapter Twenty

It was a particularly bright morning and with it, came a surge of energy for Samantha. Richard was out for a run, so Samantha, alone in the house, sought the best way to use her energy. She went into the kitchen to clean. A woman came once a week to clean the apartment, but Samantha made herself useful by making the surfaces sparkle. She made a mental note, acknowledging that it was her best morning since coming to Aruba. She awoke with no emotional baggage and it felt good. When the phone in the living-room rang, she walked briskly to it and picked it up. It was from the Aruba Police precinct. The call was for her. O'Brian had asked to speak with her.

This piece of news dampened her energy. She sat down on the couch with a rag in her left hand. Why had O'Brian asked to speak with her? He abducted and talked to her for over four hours some nights ago, so what else did he have to share? She reasoned that he must have disturbed the police enough for them to put a call through to her. Samantha earnestly awaited Richard's return, so she could tell him.

Richard didn't want her to go alone when she told him. Samantha couldn't understand why.

"It's not like anything is going to happen, Richard, the police will be there to watch over me."

Richard sighed. "Sometimes, I forget you're not a baby and that you've been living your life alone and taking care of yourself. Please go well. We will speak about it when you return."

"Sure."

After she had bathed and was ready to leave the house, she saw Richard waiting in the living room, dressed up. "At least, I can drive you to the police station," he said.

She smiled and shook her head. They walked out together and into the car.

"Do you, maybe, want to grab a bite first?" Richard asked her as he gunned the Mustang along the highway.

"No, I can never be able to eat now."

Richard understood she was excited.

"What if he has a different story regarding Ash's death?" he asked.

"I won't be too surprised," Samantha said. "I'm sure he'd do anything he can to avoid jail for abducting me. He's a smart guy."

"Is that who you are?"

"What do you mean?" Samantha gave him a quizzical look.

"Sapiosexual?"

Samantha thought about it, frowning. "You know I never thought about it. I must admit brilliance and class are turn-ons for me. But sapiosexual, no, the term is too exclusive. They are supposed to fuck people just because they're intelligent, right? Intelligence is not enough." Samantha was thinking about Peter. He was the smartest teacher and had consistently won the best teacher award in her school. He had even once taken the honors for the State Award. But she would never lay with him. Yuck!

"Why do you love me?" Richard asked seriously. "Em, do you even love me?"

"Really?" Samantha asked. The question embarrassed her to no end. Yes, she loved him. Well, she thought she did. But they just were not meant to fall in love, so it was a subject she didn't want to speak about. In fact, she didn't want to think about it.

"Eh, tell me," Richard said.

"I thought we were talking about sapiosexuality here. So, your question should be why do I fuck you?"

"Oh dear!"

"Now that's one question I have no answer to, sorry."

Richard sighed. They spent the rest of the journey in silence.

Samantha was the center of attraction as she stepped into the precinct. She thought the only thing missing from her epic entrance was an array of crazy paparazzi struggling for the best shot. She understood why everyone would stop what they were doing to look at her. She had drama, attention, and action written all over her. In the past ten days, she had been abducted and had to be at the police station. She had been the reason why a policeman got arrested. And only five days back, a woman had shot herself in the head and she had been a key-witness. And now, a man standing trial had requested to see her.

And oh, she was the sister of the murdered Ashley Blackwell, the central figure in this maze.

Samantha was led to the police interview room. "Please make yourself at home," the female officer, who led her there, said.

Samantha settled on a seat. "Are you going to be listening to what he'd tell me?"

"I can't answer that, ma'am," the officer said politely and left.

Samantha preened herself and waited. The door opened and O'Brian was led in, his hands and legs chained. He looked different. Samantha thought he had been suffering. He badly needed a shave and his cheek appeared to have lost a lot of flesh.

"Is he always in these chains?" Samantha asked the male officer that led him in.

"No, it's for your own safety."

Samantha said nothing. She watched O'Brian, who seemed to be interested in nothing else but her. After he sat opposite her at the other side of the table, Samantha asked, "Have they not been treating you well?"

"They try," O'Brian said.

"You look..." She searched for the right word. "You look—"

"Sammy, I'm in jail. I'm just not happy, that's all."

"All right."

They sat there and stared at each other. The officer that brought him in excused himself.

"You've asked to see me," Samantha said.

"Yes."

"You must have something to share then."

"Yes."

"Whatever it is, understand that they may be listening to this conversation."

"I'd be surprised if they weren't."

"Good."

O'Brian stared at her for another sixty seconds without giving a remote impression that he wanted to talk. Samantha wondered if she was to read signs or hidden texts from his face. She didn't want to rush him, so she sat there and waited.

"After we broke up, Sammy," O'Brian began, "I began by blaming myself. And then, I told myself we would work our ways back to each other after a month. We didn't. I tried. You were not interested. I gave it three months. Still didn't work out."

He chuckled slightly.

"So, Sammy, I chose to live a different life; a life without you. It would be a year later that I thought to myself I was the victim here. Yes, Ash's victim. She never really liked me, never really liked my body or anything. She just wanted to get back at you. Perhaps, for something you did to her in the past. After that mishap, I mean you catching us in bed, Ash never spoke to me again. No calls. No texts. Nothing. So, I knew she used me. She didn't want a relationship. She didn't even want the sex. I felt stupid at first. And then, anger took over me. I wanted to hurt Ash badly for hurting me. For hurting us. So, I began to search for her."

Samantha sat listening; wondering if there was going to be an end to the mystery surrounding Ash's death.

"It was not easy finding her," O'Brian said, "but when I found her, I couldn't hurt her. I wanted something more. I wanted to get back to you. So, I assumed she would help. You know, help repair what she damaged. She could easily say no. I didn't want to put myself in a position where I would be rejected, so I sought to be more convincing with my approach. Fortunately, Ash provided a leeway. She was seeing a lot of men then, while still married to her husband. I simply took photos of her and these men. Pretty compromising photos. The photos were meant to persuade her to help me."

"Like blackmail?"

"You could call it that, but I never wanted anything malicious. All I wanted was to get back to you."

"Such noble cause," Samantha said.

O'Brian sighed. "Sammy, I'm going to need you to concentrate. We are going so deep. Where we are going you don't know, but surely, sarcasm won't help you."

Samantha frowned.

"So, I met Ash and told her my intention. Not surprising, she didn't want the photos made public. And that was what I wanted. She agreed to help."

Samantha was thinking, *But he had told me this before.*

"But she couldn't help. She said she tried to get you to listen to her, but you didn't want to. I thought she didn't try enough. I called her mean and wicked and heartless. I called her all these things and told her she deserved more. And then, I said I hope she fucking burns in hell for ruining your happiness and mine. To my surprise, Sammy, Ash broke down in front of me and wept. I thought I'd never see her do that. I thought she was just a mean bitch. But Ash cried for an hour. Her body shook so much I thought she was going to die."

Samantha couldn't imagine Ash crying that much. What O'Brian was now describing to her was not her sister.

"It was incredible," O'Brian said. "I felt for her. I thought I would forever hate that bitch, but no, at that point, I only wanted to reach out to her. I cuddled her and managed to get her to stop crying. What happened next was the most unbelievable thing I thought would ever happen. Ash told me her story."

Samantha sat up in her seat. Her eyes flew wide; *Ash told you what? Ash never shared her story with anyone. No one was worthy enough to hear it!*

Samantha sat and listened in disbelief as O'Brian took her on a ride she never imagined she'd be on.

\*\*\*

Five hours later, Samantha entered her hotel room and went to lie on the bed. She curled into herself, a fetal posture, and wept.

It was important for her to spend this moment alone. She didn't want Richard to interrupt it. She was too volatile for human company now. Her phone beside her was turned off. This moment would be to the memory of Ash and her life alone.

# Chapter Twenty-One

The Oxford Home had room for only American citizens to adopt kids. The management scrutinized all paperwork and checked every address and citizenship status before approving request for adoption. When the Curtises, Jimmy and Amelia, applied to be considered to adopt a female child of no more than four, this was no different. Their papers were looked into and they were found qualified. The little adorable Lara was the reward for their effort.

But the management of Oxford Home was not to know that nothing in the paperwork they approved was true. The Curtises had taken away the little child on stolen identity. This was not to be discovered, never. Even if it was, the Curtises were miles away from the United States. They were not the Curtises, they were the Jacksons, and so were untraceable. And Mexico was their home.

Andre and Melissa Jackson loved their daughter. To them, she was not adopted. She was theirs. And they told the friends and families this much. They named her Rose. She was their rose. Four-year-old Rose was a delight. She was by far the most adorable kid in her new neighborhood in Matamoros. Her hair, now black, was dyed by Melissa to get her to look as close to her as possible, was the longest for a kid her age.

It was true that Melissa couldn't have kids. Andre supported her and together, they conceived this plan and now, she had her daughter. Melissa was, by then, in her thirties. Rose grew up like the normal kids; attending school and playing with her mates. Andre took care of her. He was a business man. He exported logs to the United States and profit from that was huge. He would take Rose to the harbor and would carry her on his shoulders, introducing her to every worker who cared to pay attention. "The heir to my throne," he'd say every time.

Rose grew up loved. She couldn't think of any privileges she was denied. So, when things changed at home, she was most affected by it. It began in her early teenage years.

It was nothing when her father began returning late from work most days. He simply gave genuine excuses and talked about how they needed a bigger house and he was working to build a mansion. Melissa would accept the excuses and would not bother him much. And then, the genuine reasons disappeared. He would simply return and go to bed, ignoring his waiting wife and the food served. Rose wasn't too bothered by this. But when the man began to stay away from home some days, she knew there was trouble.

Andre still called her his princess and took her to the harbor sometimes. He still said she was the heir to his throne and that his mansion was for her, but there was a growing disconnection between them. This disconnection was fueled by the irregularity in their communication and the tears her mother shed at night when Andre failed to show up. Andre said they were business trips, but even she knew her father's business didn't need him to travel.

Rose began to hear the raised voices. Melissa said there was another woman. At first, Andre forbade her from saying such nonsense, and then he didn't forbid her anymore. He simply said she should be content with being the main woman in his life. Rose could feel her mother losing her spark. Bitterness and anger and a sense of loss were eating at her.

One night, she awoke to hear her screaming at him, imploring him to bring the woman home; that way, she would at least get to see him, and he wouldn't have to be away from his daughter. Rose dreaded the thought of waking up to see another woman in their home. She liked her life the way it was.

But it happened. A woman did show up in their home. It was after they had moved to a new house, the mansion Andre spoke about, with its two living rooms and two kitchens. Andre gave the woman a room. It was obvious Andre had carefully planned this. The new house had five rooms. Melissa had one. Rose, one. Andre took one and the new woman was allotted one. The last room was reserved for guests. Rose couldn't get used to the new set-up. Andre told her everything would be all right. Even when he made her dress-up as a little bride for the marriage ceremony with the second wife, Rose thought her family had become a joke. Nothing was going to be all right.

Peace and respite lasted in the home for a while. Melissa tried as much as possible to stay in her lane. She avoided crossing paths with the new wife, and most importantly, she didn't try to over-assert herself in the home. She was a good woman, Rose thought, and she was a great lover of peace.

One day, she asked her mother if she was going to leave Andre. Melissa had no such plans. Andre stayed with her, she told Rose, even when she was medically damaged. He could have left her, but he didn't, so she wasn't going to leave him because his errant libido took hold of him. Rose wondered what the medical condition was but Melissa told her she was too young to understand.

Peace and respite didn't last. Andre began to physically abuse Melissa. The new wife was pregnant, so Andre pampered her. When she told Andre that Melissa had shoved her and that she had fallen to the ground, Andre was enraged. She accused Melissa of being envious and called her names, which included 'barren.' But the new wife had simply lied. Andre wouldn't hear it. It was that day that he first raised his hand against Melissa. But it never stopped with that day.

*It never really stops with the first day.* That Tashika, she was such a bloody liar, Rose knew. She lied all the time about Melissa and Andre fell for them. Rose thought the woman made her father stupid. As her belly grew bigger, Andre became more stupid. Melissa took Rose and left the house. Andre didn't come for them, he didn't care. He had a new heir growing in Tashika's belly.

Quite easily, Rose became a sad teenager. It wasn't difficult. No longer was she that privileged kid from a loving home, she was the teenager from a split home. And more importantly, life was hard now. Melissa and Rose found it difficult to make it on their own without Andre's input. And Melissa was never going to ask Andre for anything; he had made his choice.

Rose would hawk fruits in the streets, while her mother sold fruits and veggies in a small store. They hardly made enough money. Rose withdrew from the private school she was attending and enrolled in a government-assisted school. This didn't sadden her as much as days when she'd be on the street hawking and Andre would drive past in his fine car. On such days, she would weep and go to bed somber.

But Rose had peace of mind. No longer were she and Melissa scared of Andre's return from work in the evening, because then, Tashika would have a lie waiting to feed him. But Rose returned home one evening to find her mother bloodied. She ran to her, scared, alarmed. Andre was in the house, her mother told her, and they had had an argument.

Rose couldn't take the fact that Andre would, after watching them leave his house, come over to their tattered apartment to beat her mother up. She was enraged. She wished she had enough strength to face him. But she would get her opportunity in a way that she didn't expect.

Just three months later, she returned to find her mother screaming. Andre was there again to beat her up. Rose ran into the kitchen. Her eyes settled on the kitchen knife. She gripped the handle and ran back into the room.

All she wanted to do was just get him off her mother. She didn't even realize where she stabbed him. Her eyes had been closed. Andre bled to death.

Rose, innocent and naïve, was, now, guilty of murder. She was fifteen.

# Chapter Twenty-Two

"It is important that you do not panic. It's important you remain focused. Don't let emotions and guilt ruin you. See what happened here, you didn't do it. What did I say? You didn't do it. Say after me, 'I didn't do it. I didn't do it.' Good. I did it. I, your mother, Melissa, was the one who did it. Repeat after me, 'My mother killed him.' Good. Good. I killed him."

These were Melissa's words to Rose. Melissa had held her, cuddled her, and stopped her from screaming and running outside the house. She told Rose it was her fault that this happened and that she must take responsibility for it. She would never live to see her daughter go to jail. The crime was not of Rose's making, but rather a product of the stupidity of two adults.

"Don't ever tell any human that you killed your own father!"

Rose wept. She wept because she had taken a life; because of the image in her head of Andre's body jerking, while blood pumped out of his body; of the fact that her mother, as innocent of the crime as she was, was going to take responsibility for it. She wept because she was losing the two most important people in her life, the only people she ever loved, in one day. She wept because the future she saw, without them, was bleak.

Melissa called the police. Rose listened to her tell them that her husband was dead and that she had killed him with her hands. Rose's heart broke. She was there when the police arrived and took Melissa away. She was broken beyond words.

Rose would cry for days, mourn her mother, and be depressed. She would become sickly. And one day, left alone in the house, she picked up the same knife that ended her father's life and sliced her wrist. She awoke two days later in a hospital bed. Tashika was the first face she saw.

"I guess we ended up together," Tashika said. "Who would have thought that?"

Tashika was officially her step-mother and guardian now. She took her home and offered her her old room. The room where her father had come to sit at the foot of her bed to talk to her. She would be haunted for a long time, until she complained to Tashika to move her. Tashika snorted. She did nothing.

Rose was not reregistered back in school. Tashika gave the excuse that the teenager was volatile and needed to be consistently watched. And that she didn't trust the school to do that. Tashika never really watched Rose.

One year later, Tashika sold Andre's houses and relocated to Real de Catorce. Here, there was a man waiting for her. She remarried him and Rose moved in with them. Rose hated that she was not enrolled into any school and as such, she was mostly somber. Tashika and her new husband would say to her, "The world is in trouble, you look bitterer than that murdering mother of yours."

Tashika opened businesses. There was the restaurant, the local bar, and the brewing company. She invested hugely all the money she inherited from Andre. The businesses were well-run, so Tashika was growing richer every day. Even Rose had to admit she was a good businesswoman. What she couldn't understand, however, was why she couldn't send her to school. Rose was, instead, made to work for Tashika. She worked in all three of her companies, depending on how Tashika wanted to use her at any point in time. Rose never got paid for the jobs she did. Nor the ones she would do in the future.

At seventeen, Rose blossomed into a beautiful woman. She was nubile and elegant. And it wasn't too surprising when she caught the interest of one of Tashika's potential investors at the brewery. All he needed to be convinced to invest in her business was Rose's body. Tashika pimped Rose off to him. The man was fifty-nine. Rose lost her virginity to him.

Rose's days seemed to grow dimmer as she aged. Tashika had no issue shipping her off to whoever was going to bring cash. Rose served her purpose, for which, there was no personal benefit to her. There was going to be no succor for her. More men got interested in her and Tashika did them the honors.

Even Tashika's husband had his round with her. Tashika made it too clear to him that she was too tired for sex and encouraged him to have his way with Rose. The goat, he did. He took Rose several times from the back, pounding her mercilessly with penis the size of a pestle.

Rose was consistently depressed. But she was not going to try to kill herself anymore. When Diego, a twenty-two-year-old driver, came into her life, it was the temporary respite Rose needed. Diego was different from the men who had ravaged her. He cared about her. He tried to uplift her. She told him to take her away, that with Tashika, she was lost and useless. Diego did. They went away to Chihuahua. There, she sought succor. But succor was a long way from coming. Diego left her after two months and traveled to the United States. Rose was again lost and without means to feed herself.

The landlord wanted his rent. Rose could not afford it. But more importantly, she could not afford to return to Tashika. The landlord found a way out. For regular sex, whenever he wanted, her rent was waived. Rose let him through. She had had sex with Tashika's men without gain. Her landlord was a beast. He was randy every time. During her period, he didn't mind, he still thrust home, marveling at how the blood made her a lot more accessible. Rose was disgusted by the act each time.

Rose began to walk the red district lane. To feed, to make plans to get away from her situation, she needed money. She didn't know of anything else to do but to walk the red district, seeing to the needs of different men. She would return home and weep and grew depressed with the thought of how different her life was from what she had wanted it to be.

Perhaps, this life just wasn't for her. Perhaps, she wasn't created to be tangible. Perhaps, it was time to end it all, and see if there was something for her in the afterlife. But she needed to see her mother again.

Few months to her twentieth birthday, Rose traveled to see Melissa. Mother and child held each other tightly and cried their eyes out. They had both changed remarkably. While Melissa had aged and dwindled and faded, Rose was now a beautiful woman. But Melissa couldn't help but notice the glaring hooded look, the shades of her eyes, and the pain they harbored. She cried for her daughter.

"I can't keep up anymore, Mother, I can't," Rose told her mother in tears. "I do not think I have long to live."

Melissa forbade her from speaking such ill and that she didn't suffer to be in jail so she could throw her life away. She said she knew Tashika could never take care of Rose and told her that there could be hope for her in America.

"Find your real mother there," she advised Rose.

Rose was shocked. She could never have imagined that Melissa was not her real mother.

Melissa told her of the medical condition that inhibited her from bearing children and how she had traveled to the United States with Andre and adopted her.

"Your real name is Rose Stamp. You were adopted from The Oxford Home. It shouldn't be too difficult to find."

Rose left the prison with the revelation that shattered her life in more ways than it mended it.

# Chapter Twenty-Three

It left Rose with so much disappointment; the barrage of rejections. It hurt her so bad to know that she had a real mother who gave her away at the age of four. She was never loved; she was never good enough to be wanted. And it was the same case for her father. Once he was able to impregnate another woman, knowing that within the walls of her womb lay his true seed, he abandoned her. He never really loved her enough.

Rose met Hugo. Melissa had said he was the immigration agent that helped her and Andre get the visa they needed to travel to the United States. He was so crooked at this that he got them stolen identities, one with which she and her husband used to acquire Rose.

Hugo was ready to help her for a five-thousand-dollar token. Rose paid with Melissa's stone, the one that remained in her jewelry box while she was married to Andre. She gave Hugo but one recommendation, "Change my name to Ash; Ashley in full."

Rose knew it was the right thing to do. Rose was a symbol of love, yet no one loved her enough to care about her, to want to have and keep her. The name was dead to her. She had been through a lot, so it was symbolic enough she named herself Ash. It resonated with her life better. Life had burned her without mercy or favor. Ash was just so fitting.

Once Ash made it into the United States, finding her mother was not difficult. She watched to house to see how the Stamps lived in her absence. She saw Samantha and was stupefied. The beauty of her! The grace! She was a student. Ash followed her everywhere. She thought Samantha looked lovely and would make a sweet sister. But she had everything that was denied Ash. Education. Freedom. Privilege. Food and shelter, gotten without raising a finger to work, without sitting on a man and grinding him until his was saturated with satisfaction.

The first thing Ash did was to destroy the bathroom pipes of the Stamps' apartment. That was before she showed up in their home. Samantha remembered how it freaked her mother out that anyone could be malicious enough to destroy their pipes. They had to call the plumber. It took two days to fix them. They were distressed in those two days. Ash had her reason for destroying the pipes. Before she traveled to meet Melissa, she had been living in a room where the toilet pipes didn't function and she had to use public toilet and wait until late at night or in the early hours of the morning to bath outside.

Ash finally revealed herself to Samantha and her mother on a Sunday afternoon. They had been making salad and really talking loudly and happily when the door opened wide. Ash stood at the doorway staring at them. She just stood there. For some reasons, neither she nor her mother moved. They just stared back at her.

Samantha had stared at her; intrigued by their remarkable resemblance. She wanted to talk to her, to ask her what she wanted, but she just couldn't say anything. She would later know that her mother had recognized Ash right away and she knew who she was. She had been too stunned to move. Then Ash walked in and sat down.

"I see you're all living comfortably," was the first thing she said.

Rose burst out in tears. Samantha was lost. How was she to know? Her mother never mentioned that there was another child. When Rose had cried her fill and moved to cuddle and touch Ash, she had simply said, her voice cold, "Don't touch me!"

From that day, it was easy to see Ash hadn't come to make peace and bond with her new family; she had simply come to pay them back for the things she suffered. Samantha had welcomed her, had embraced her, and given her substance to her, but Ash was only ready to share a modicum of her misery around.

\*\*\*

Samantha lay in bed curled up, weeping for the sister she never knew. She wished Ash had shared her story. They would have understood her better. They'd have loved her unconditionally. And, perhaps, she wouldn't have been dead and gone like she now was.

"I am so sorry, Ash. I should have been there for you. I should have opened myself enough to earn your trust. And now it's too late."

Samantha cried for her for hours.

It was around 10:00 p.m. that she got up from the bed and went into the bathroom. She stripped and climbed into the bath-tub. She let warm water from the shower wash her body. She stayed still. It was her hope that it would wash away her melancholy and the stain she felt was perched on her body from not being of any help to Ash. When she was done with this ritual, she dried her body and went back to the room, her clothes in her hand. She got into them.

Samantha wanted to call her mother to share what she had discovered about Ash, but she was scared she'd sound too broken and that she was going to go through another round of crying. Her eyes hurt from the tears she shed.

She picked up her phone from the bed and turned it on. The S.M.S began flying in, her phone vibrated as they entered one after the other. There were twenty-eight SMS in all. They were from Richard. He wanted to know where she was. He was scared for her. He didn't know what to do. He had called the cops.

Samantha typed a message back to him, 'Come get me, I'm at the hotel.'

She sat waiting for Richard. She needed him now. Maybe he could help her stop feeling too bad, too down. O'Brian had been too detailed with his story. It was pretty graphic to Samantha. And now, every detail, every image was lodged in her head. O'Brian had even promised to let her listen to the recording, because, according to him, he got too overwhelmed with the story and decided to record the ending part. He wanted Samantha to listen to it, to hear her sister's voice, so she could believe it was her story indeed. Samantha had no doubt it was Ash's story, all right. If it wasn't, O'Brian couldn't possibly have known of the damaged pipes in their house when Samantha was only sixteen years old.

But she had no intention of listening to Ash's voice. In the state in which O'Brian described her, Ash's voice would probably leave her shattered. She didn't think she could survive more hurt or sadness than she already was doing.

A frantic knock came from the door. It was about seventeen minutes since she called Richard and so she knew he'd be the one. She rose from her bed and opened the door. It was Richard. He hugged and squeezed her. He held her off, looked at her, and then squeezed her again.

"Oh Sam, I was so, so scared for you."

Samantha hugged him back. She held on tightly. Richard held her off and walked her to the bed. He was in a haste to know what happened to her.

"You look so… so drained, Sam. What's going on? What happened?"

Samantha didn't know where to start.

"I've called the police several times. They had no idea where you were. I was not buying that. I told them all I knew was that they invited you over and it was up to them to make you available. I've threatened them. I've briefed my lawyer. I have—"

"Richard, can you take me home?"

Richard was confused. He stared at Samantha; sadness registering in his eyes.

"To your house, I mean."

Richard breathed easier. "Let's go then."

He helped her up and led her out of the room.

They drove in silence until Richard saw the lights of a restaurant come into view. "Can we get something to eat? I haven't had anything but breakfast all day."

Samantha hadn't had food all day. "Yes, let's get something."

Richard pulled into the restaurant. "What would you like?"

"Doesn't matter."

Richard shrugged and got out of the car. Samantha waited in the car. The restaurant was classy. *It looked so much like the restaurant where Ash duped her of her money,* she thought and wondered if everything would remind her of Ash now.

Richard returned and placed the food in the back-seat of the car. "I got pasta and salmon and coke for you."

Samantha said nothing.

"I was so confused there and then I remembered you mentioned you had a thing for that combination, so I got it."

"Thank you." She managed a smile.

Richard pulled back into the road. Back in the house, he helped Samantha get out of the car. Then he took her into the house before returning for the food. Samantha wondered if he was now treating her like she was disabled.

They ate in the living room. Samantha ate very little. Richard emptied his plate in minutes. It was easy to see he was famished. Samantha thought it was her fault, as he couldn't bring himself to eat with her missing.

When they were done, Richard cleared the table. He returned and sat in the same seat as Samantha.

"What now?" he asked.

"The problem is where to start," Samantha said.

"I will be fine with your choice, Sam."

Samantha inhaled deeply. "It happens that Ash is a product of her struggles."

"What do you mean?"

"O'Brian knows Ash's story. I mean, from the very beginning."

Richard frowned.

"Ash told him."

"She told him? They weren't even close." He thought about it. "Or were they?"

"They weren't. They never were. But, somehow, he happened to be the one who found Ash in her most vulnerable state. Ash told him all. It is the most exhilarating thing I ever heard."

Richard sat up and readied himself for what was coming: The Tales of Ash.

Samantha turned fully to face him. "Did you love Ash?"

Richard frowned at the turn of things. "Em... yes!"

"Enough?"

"Em..."

"Or you just enjoyed fucking her?"

Richard's jaw fell. It would have been great if Samantha's tone was hard. It would have indicated she was upset from the tales she heard of her sister. But here, she was not; she was sober and calm and logical. It was worse than her being upset.

"You never loved her enough, Richard. You never did. We all failed Ash. If we didn't, she might have had enough warmth and comfort in our company to share her story. One of us might have saved her."

Richard had nothing to say.

Samantha rose and took the stairs. "Good night."

Richard was stunned. She knew Samantha was right. He never really loved Ash enough. Perhaps, it all started with the way she deceived him. He wished that hadn't happened. They might have had a different love-diagram. But he was worried now. He couldn't tell how this would affect his relationship with Samantha. He wanted to know what she knew... What that O'Brian swindler told her.

He called the police station. His call was directed to the commander in-charge. "I have found Samantha," he said. "She was in a hotel room, resting."

"Good," the commander, Commander Huffman, said.

"She is traumatized and can't talk. I am worried for her sake."

"I am sorry about that," the commander said sincerely.

"May I come in and speak with that O'Brian guy? I need to know what he told her; that way I might be able to help her."

"Oh, we released O'Brian on bail this evening."

Richard was shocked. "What?"

"After going through—"

"He abducted my girl—my dead wife's sister!"

"We know that much. But it turned out he never really had any malicious intent. He simply wanted to share her late sister's message with her."

"Ash dropped a message for her?"

"Not really. It was for him. Anyway, we've reviewed it all and decided to grant him bail. The lady, Samantha, also wanted him released and all charges dropped." The commander was saying something about Richard coming in

177

in the morning for detailed briefing when Richard dropped the call.

Richard's head spun. What had that O'Brian told Samantha? He took the stairs and made his way to the guest room. He needed to know. It was important to him. Ash was his wife, too.

Samantha was in bed, sleeping soundly. He watched her for some time. Then he walked over, undressed himself, and got into bed next to her, cuddling her, and listening to her light breathing.

# Chapter Twenty-Four

Richard was in the kitchen drinking a cup of coffee. He needed as much of it as he could get. This was his second cup. Samantha had just shared Ash's story with him after waking up to find him next to her. He wondered if Ash was willing to share her story with him, when she told him she wasn't willing to go on with the divorce, that there was something he needed to understand. He had simply thought Ash wanted to eat his cake and have it.

*Maybe… if he had loved her more. Or pretended better.*

Samantha came into the kitchen wearing his shirt only, the one he shed in her room last night. Strangely, he liked that she wore it. It reassured him that she may not hate him for not loving Ash enough. He had been so scared last night, when she talked about it.

"I thought you were going to get coffee for both of us?" Samantha said with a teasing tone.

"I was. I'm sorry. I just couldn't bring myself to function without drinking enough of it."

Samantha went over to the kettle and poured a cup for herself. She closed her eyes as she sipped. "Coffee is life some times," she said.

"You know I was thinking, we may have gotten it all wrong with Ash, it's a blame we should shoulder. But there is something good we can do."

"What's that?"

"We could find Melissa, Ash's mother in Mexico, and see how she is doing."

"Oh!"

"She is only in jail for ten years, yes, which means she's been out about three years now. We may find how she is faring and see how we may help her."

Samantha thought about it. Her eyes lightened up. "I saw a woman at Ash's grave two days ago. She should be in her fifties."

Richard's eyes narrowed. "I don't know any fifty to sixty-year-old who would be at Ash's grave. We didn't keep such circle of acquaintances."

"She fits into Ash's mum's age bracket," Samantha said. "She even said she knew Ash. And yes, she called her Rose."

"That's Ash's mum!" Richard announced like it was some victory.

"Sadly," said Samantha, "she didn't give me her number. I was going to get it, but she took mine instead."

"Oh, dear. I hope she calls. I hope we can be able to help her."

"And console her," Samantha said sadly. Before now, she hadn't taken a moment to think of how heart-broken Ash's mum might be after leaving jail, only to never see her daughter again. She thought her consolation for spending ten years for the girl she loved would have been the girl waiting at the exit-gate to embrace her. Now, death news was all she had.

"I hope she calls," Richard said, "though I will run a few searches myself."

"I want to go to the room and call my mum. I figure it will be the longest call I ever made."

"I will be in my room," Richard said.

Samantha left the kitchen.

It would be nearly two hours later before Samantha heard Richard knock on her door. He entered. "Did I interrupt anything?"

"Definitely not the call," Samantha said. "I finished a long time ago."

"I need food in my body. What do you suggest? We order or we go out to eat?"

"How about we cook?"

Richard flinched. It was a weird question. The only thing his kitchen was used for was to brew coffee. It took him a while to realize Samantha was only joking.

"Let's eat out," she said.

"Get ready then."

In the car, Richard asked her, "If you saw that woman you ran into at the graveyard, would you know her?"

"Melissa? Yes."

"I feel personally like I owe her."

Samantha remained quiet. It was the same way Ash felt. It was that feeling; the indebtedness to her mother that drove her crazy. This was the part of the story she had kept away from Richard. She didn't know how he'd react to it. Imagine telling him that Ash never loved him from day one and that she only got into marriage with him because she wanted to milk him and to use him as a way into the circle of the wealthy. It would shatter him. He would further lose trust in humans, seeing how Eric and his wife had betrayed him.

Ash never loved Richard. O'Brian told her that. Ash had told him that.

"Why, then, are you married to him?" O'Brian had asked her.

Ash had a long, convincing explanation. When she left Mexico, she knew she'd return. She had two things she knew she'd do before her death. She needed to compensate Melissa and make her remaining years on earth better and she needed to pay Tashika back for all the terrible things she made her go through.

But Ash could never be able to do any of these. She lacked the education to land a well-paying job and she had no cash to set up a profiting business. So, Ash was stuck. And time was running out.

When Richard showed up, he had the answer Ash needed. She wedded him. The year they wedded was the year Melissa was released from jail. She never called Melissa, never got in touch, but she knew the calculations. She figured it was pointless getting in touch with Melissa, until she was ready to compensate her for the years lost. So, Ash was under self-induced pressure.

She could not really get any finances from Richard to carry out her wish. Richard kept his money well. Only he knew the pins to the credit cards. He didn't withhold gifts from her, but she just never had access to his money.

So, Ash kept on needing more gifts. Clothes. Bags. Shoes. Jewelry. She had them all. She figured she'd sell them when she was ready to travel back to Mexico. It was a cool plan. So, seemingly, Ash had more things than she needed.

The revenues from the gift would be a long haul from Ash's plans. Tashika had become a wealthy woman in Mexico, so Ash needed to be a bigger fish to challenge. That was when the promiscuity began. Ash knew the men who were wealthy. She knew who to flirt with, who to fuck, and who to ignore. She had been in the circle. There was Eric Marshall, the Regional Manager of a bank. There was Saint Cruise, the perfumes mogul from Canada. There was Jonathan Kent. He owned a clothing line that was the in-fashion. There were all these men. Ash knew them. She knew their weaknesses; the things they had in common.

They all respected their wives and were keen to avoid scandals. Now, if they didn't like scandals, why fuck with Ash in the first place?

It was simple. Ash presented herself as a woman who had more to lose than they did. She was married and would be penniless if their sex-scandal ever blew open.

Ash was a woman on a mission. She slept with these men. She kept the affairs secret. She was never after their money. She had her own money. Or so they thought. When Ash had these men where she wanted them, with proves of affairs and the timelines, she sprung a shocker on them. She was pregnant!

Now, it was all right if Ash was pregnant. These men knew the best doctors who could arrange a secluded VIP dilation and curettage on her, but Ash didn't just want an abortion. She wanted a million dollars!

There were five men. Sure, they were all capable of paying up. And Ash was going to divorce Richard. The amount of money would be huge in the end. Ash was going to achieve her purpose. But this game of hers proved too dangerous. She hadn't considered the scorn of an aggrieved woman. Margaret Marshall put to rest Ash and her scheming.

O'Brian said he had been torn by Ash's scheming that he didn't know if he was to empathize with her or call her names. In the end, he said he understood her better and he was appreciative of how strong she was. He wished she could get a grip over her obsession with what she wanted in Mexico, as life could be more enjoyable that way.

He had been too shocked to hear of her death. He wished he had not been too weak to talk her out of the dangerous path she walked. By the time he was done talking, he and Samantha were soaked in their own tears.

***

"Oh, an Italian restaurant?" Samantha said.

Richard nodded. "Yes, in honor of Ash."

They strolled down to a seat by the window and sat down. A waiter came around as soon as they were settled. Samantha placed the order.

"For both of us," she said.

"Hey, allow me to choose mine," Richard said.

Samantha made the waiter go away. "I didn't argue when you made my order last night, did I?"

"I seem to remember you saying something like, actually something as precise as, 'Doesn't matter.'"

"That's a figment of your own imagination," Samantha said and suppressed a laugh.

After their food was served, Samantha only ate a little when her phone rang. She took the call. There was silence from the other side. And then the connection went dead. Samantha thought that was weird. She shrugged and resumed eating.

"So I was thinking, as a way to help you relieve the stress of these past few days, that we visit the spa," Richard said. "Feel free to say no, if it isn't your thing. But the offer is on the ta—"

"Oh my God!" Samantha said excitedly. "That was Melissa! It was Melissa that just called me."

"Melissa?"

"I don't know. I mean, I'm not sure, she never said anything when she called. But I'm convinced I can't be wrong. It's her!" She started to get up. "Let's go."

Richard frowned. "Wait. Why?"

"Let's go!"

"Where are we going to?"

"I don't know. The graveyard, I think."

Samantha was already angling away from the table.

"Wait a minute!" Richard said. "I need to settle the bill."

Moments later, Richard was on the highway, speeding to the graveyard. At the entrance, Samantha told Richard to park the car. "I'm going in alone."

"Any reason for that?"

"If Melissa is there, then I'd like to talk to her. I wouldn't want the presence of another person to off-set her."

"Ash was my wife."

"No one is arguing that. Just park the car and wait."

Samantha eased herself out of the car. She could tell Richard was shooting arrows in her small back using his glare. Samantha made her way inside the graveyard. It was still a long way from where Ash's grave was, so she tried to hurry up.

Melissa was there, all right. Samantha couldn't tell who it was that was standing there with her back to her, but it possibly couldn't be any other than Melissa.

It was Melissa, all right.

Samantha walked up to where she stood looking at the grave. There were so many flowers there now. Samantha wondered if anyone else but Melissa was bringing some as well. Both women stood side-by-side, not talking, not looking at each other.

After a few minutes, Samantha turned to her.

"How are you?" she asked.

"Devastated. Shredded so much I doubt I am still human."

Samantha wanted to hug her. She saw her eyes become misty. There was no telling the amount of pain in this woman's heart.

"I'm sorry," she said, "I really am very sorry."

Tears welled down Melissa's cheek now. "I could have done things differently. I could have saved this poor child."

"I'm sure you did the things you thought right."

"I didn't. I was foolish. I could have made better plans, seen the future, saved her from what she was becoming. I feel so responsible."

"We are all responsible. We could have done more."

Melissa tried to stop sobbing.

"How did you know of her death? You called her Rose the other day, yet here you are, standing over Ash Blackwell's gravestone."

"I was informed."

Samantha frowned. No one knew who Ash's adoptive mother was.

"A man named O'Brian Clooney called me. I don't know how he found me, but he said he had news that might interest me. He proceeded to tell me."

"O'Brian is my friend."

Melissa was no longer crying now.

"How is life in Mexico?" Samantha asked.

"It is difficult. Nothing is as it used to be."

"How long are you staying here?"

"As long as it takes to rid myself of this guilt I feel."

"I will be giving you a call. Maybe we can have dinner together, along with Ash's husband."

"Oh, she was married," Melissa asked; her face lit a little.

"Yes. Although they were going to get a divorce."

Melissa's face fell. "I did this."

"You did nothing, Melissa."

Intense shock registered on the woman's face. Samantha saw it.

"What's wrong? Are you okay?" she asked.

"Didn't know you knew that name."

"O'Brian told me the story yesterday, so I now know a bit about my sister. It's a shame what she had to—"

"I have to go," Melissa said, leaving.

"Oh wait!" Samantha had so many things to talk about.

Melissa didn't stop. She didn't respond. She just walked away as fast as she could. Samantha was left with a puzzled look on her face.

She returned her attention to the grave. She thought she'd never be here again, but her she was, and with a new perspective of Ash.

*I am sorry, dear sister. The world was cruel to you. No one understood you. No one cared enough to. You were alone always. May the angels embrace you and give you comfort.*

Samantha left the grave feeling better than the last time she was here. When she got out of the graveyard, Richard was gone. The car was not anywhere to be found. She knew Richard was upset for not letting him follow her to Ash's grave. She was upset that he was upset over the matter. She had thought he was mature enough to understand.

She brought out her phone and placed an Uber call. While she waited, she wondered what she did to upset Melissa. She was eager to share her experience with the woman with Richard, which made her even more upset, now that he had foolishly driven home.

Her Uber ride took only ten minutes to get to her. When the driver asked about the destination, she told him Meiz Hotel.

She was in the Uber, still slightly upset, when her phone rang. It was Richard on the line. She let the phone ring until it stopped. Richard called back. She didn't take it still. Richard was being petty by leaving her behind. The phone rang a third time. She took the call.

"I am currently at the Fetih Hotel," Richard said.

Samantha raised an eyebrow. "So?"

"Apparently, Melissa is lodged here."

Samantha frowned. She couldn't tell why this was important though.

"The Fetih hotel is one of the most expensive hotels you can find here. So, Melissa, who got out of jail three or so years ago and without a dime, can she really afford to lodge here for more than a night?"

The alarm rang clearly in Samantha's mind. She wasn't Melissa, the woman. *She was Tashika!*

"Could you take me to the Fetih Hotel instead?" Samantha said to the driver. "Sorry."

"No trouble, ma'am," the driver said.

Samantha found Richard in his car, parked some distance from the hotel. She joined him in the front seat.

"You followed her, I see," Samantha said. "Why?"

"I saw her hurrying out of the graveyard. I knew something was amidst. I ran into the graveyard to check you out. Once I saw you were standing there still, I ran back to the car and decided to follow her. She had a driver waiting. I nearly missed her."

"I checked the cost of lodging here a night. It's outrageous. You are right, Melissa can't afford it."

"So, if that is Tashika, what exactly is she doing here?"

"Let's find out." Samantha started opening the door.

"Wait. You can't just walk over to the receptionist and demand to see Tashika and then she lets you through. She'd need to call the room first and ask her if she was willing to receive some visitors who look like they want to kill her…"

"We don't want to kill her. And we don't look like we want to kill her."

"The interpretation of how we look is best left to Tashika."

"So what do we do?"

"Now we are scheming like criminals." Richard laughed.

"Focus, Richard."

"Okay. Let's go finish what we started."

"What's that?"

"Breakfast. You thought I'd forget how you yanked me away. Poor waiter, when I paid him, he thought we left because the food was shitty."

"I know. But why are we talking about breakfast right at the time we are talking about Tashika?"

"They are actually connected. We go to the restaurant to eat. We seat where we can watch the hotel lobby and entrance. We wait out Tashika. Once she shows up, we kill her."

"Richard, what's wrong with you? We are not killing anyone."

Richard laughed. "Let's go."

They left the car, crossed the road, and went into the hotel's premises. They went straight to the restaurant. Richard found a vintage seat with a good view of the hotel's entrance. They sat down and placed their orders.

"Eggs and salad for the lady and a glass of white wine, too," Richard said.

"Richard, stop kidding, I don't want any of those."

Richard tried to make the waiter go away, but he insisted on waiting to hear the order from Samantha. Samantha smiled at him and placed her order.

When they finished eating and were now sipping their wine, Richard saw Tashika emerge from the hotel. He tapped Samantha's arm and indicated that their game was here. Richard called the waiter over so they could quickly pay, but then, they saw Tashika turn and begin walking toward the restaurant. They sat back and waited.

As Tashika came through the glass door, Samantha rose and stood in her way.

"Tashika!" she hissed.

Tashika nearly had a heart-attack. Her face went wild with terror.

"You bitch!" Samantha howled and raised her hand to strike her. But Richard was quicker. He held her hand. Samantha raised the second.

"You killer!" Richard curtailed her strike.

"Let me go!" She wrestled with him. "She killed her! She killed Ash! It's all because of her."

Richard held her still. They had drawn attention to themselves now. The waiter, the cashier, and the few guests there were all staring at the exchange now.

Tashika just stood there, mortified. She looked feverish.

"Hey Sam, calm down," Richard said to her.

The waiter was over now.

"Can you take it easy please?" he said.

Samantha stopped wrestling. Richard led her back to their seat. He settled next to her. "Take it easy, Sam."

Samantha tried to calm herself down.

After a while, Tashika joined them in their seat. She sat far away from Samantha, but closer to Richard.

"I am Tashika," she said, "but you already know that. May I sit here?"

"You are already sitting here," Richard said.

"Thank you."

She looked at Samantha. Samantha could have shot her with her eyes.

"It's obvious you've heard a lot about me," Tashika said. "Everything you heard about me is true. All the names, I deserve them. I am a terrible person." She shook her head. "I was horrible to that child."

She began to cry now. She reached for tissue in her purse.

"When I think back to what I did to that child, I know I do not deserve mercy or her forgiveness." She turned to Samantha. "Nor yours. And that child did nothing to me. I wasn't even paying her back for her mother's sin, because Melissa was never mean to me. I was just a wicked woman. I had no reason. I was just wicked."

She broke down and began to cry again. "I damaged that child. I killed her. It was all me."

She cried for a long time.

"Where is Melissa?" Samantha asked coldly.

"Yes," said Richard, "we wanted to see her. To see if there is a way we could be of help to her."

Tashika began another round of crying. When she could speak, she said, "You cannot see her. Oh, Melissa, you can't."

"Why's that?" Samantha asked.

"She never made it out of prison. She died."
Samantha and Richard were horrified.

# Chapter Twenty-Five

It was still summer. Samantha wouldn't have thought in her strangest dream that she'd find herself in Mexico and she wasn't even here in search of more sun. As the car navigated the rough road, Samantha looked out of the window, trying to imagine little Ash running around these neighborhoods, living innocently with all the energy and curiosity of a child.

"It's just about ten minutes more," Tashika said, half-turning to Richard and Samantha in the backseat. She was sitting in the front seat, helping the driver with the easiest route to the central penitentiary of Santa Maria Ixcotel in the metropolitan city of Oaxaca.

Richard could tell Tashika was doing too much to please him and Samantha. He wished she could stop and just be herself. When they decided at the restaurant that they'd visit Melissa's grave, which was the least she could have wanted from Ash. Tashika had volunteered to help them get there. Samantha, of course, didn't want her help, but Tashika had insisted.

"It's so difficult for us Mexicans to get American visa," she said. "That's why there are so many illegal migrants. So, we are now making our visa a little difficult for you Americans to get. The protocols are not as easy as they used to be. I can get you visas in one day. I know the right people."

Richard and Samantha knew she was right. They didn't have time. They needed to get to Melissa's grave as quickly as they could. Tashika arranged the visas the next day and on the third, they were flying to Mexico. They boarded the same plane; Samantha said it was fine, as long as she didn't have to sit with Tashika in the plane. Tashika sat six rows behind them.

A Mercedes was waiting to take them to their hotel when they arrived. Tashika gave them her number and told them they could call when they were ready to visit the grave. She took off in an S.U.V, driven by a chauffeur.

Samantha thought their hotel-room looked great. Tashika had arranged for it and had seen to the bill. Though she had said she simply got the owner not to charge a dime. Samantha said to Richard, "You're not going to give her a call, are you?"

"Of course not," Richard said. He found the phone number of the prison where Melissa had been incarcerated and put a call across to them. Samantha went into the bathroom for a quick shower. After what seemed like ten minutes, Richard was no closer to finding what he needed. He was frustrated.

Samantha gave him a tired look when she came out of the bathroom. "What's the problem?"

"I think they're a bunch of idiots there. After making me talk to every official in that office, they ended up with burial sites being classified and restricted to only family. They needed proof that I was family."

"Classified, huh? Is that how that word gets abused around here?"

"One said I didn't even sound like I knew her. For God's sake, how was I supposed to sound?"

"Mexican."

They sat in silence for a while. Richard turned to Samantha, thinking of the best way to say what was on his mind.

"Do it," Samantha said.

Richard dialed Tashika's number. She simply told him to get ready. She'd be at his hotel in thirty minutes.

Tashika and her driver were there in less than thirty minutes. "We got to that prison right away," she said to them. "Nothing is ever too classified."

After they got to the prison, it took less than fifteen minutes for Tashika to extract the information they needed. "They'd have provided the answer quicker," she said to Samantha and Richard. "They still operate manually and had to look through loads of records. She's been dead for more than four years."

Samantha was beginning to see how powerful Tashika was. Doors opened to her. She had her foot in all the major places. She understood why Ash needed all the money she could grab in order to fight her. It was indeed going to be a huge task for Ash, and now, she wished Ash hadn't had to bother herself with such. She'd have still been alive. Even Melissa, whom Ash wanted to compensate, was long dead.

She forced herself to stop thinking these thoughts. She didn't want to cry. Not anymore.

"The graveyard is not far from here," Tashika said. "Grave number 3325. But we need to get flowers first."

Richard turned to Samantha.

"Yes, let's get flowers," Samantha said.

At the flowers store, Samantha got white lilies. Richard got red roses and pink lilies.

"The roses are more in memory of Rose," he said to Samantha. "You know, Ash. The other is for the woman who loved her so much and lost her life proving it to her."

Samantha nodded.

Tashika bought all the flowers she could find. The car's booth was filled with it. Samantha thought she was trying to free herself of the guilt she felt with flower gifts.

The graveyard was not a quiet place. Perhaps, it could manage to be, but not today. There were about four burials going on here simultaneously. Samantha thought of the fickleness of life and how every individual at the burial ceremonies would mourn their different dead for different reasons.

Tashika led the way, struggling to keep her flowers from scattering in the wind. Richard followed behind somberly. Samantha wondered what was on his mind. Was he thinking of the fickleness of life as well?

Tashika stopped in front of the grave. It was grave number 3325 with the name Melissa Jackson written on it. Richard stopped beside her. Samantha joined them, forming a row of three.

Seeing the grave had a melting effect on Samantha's heart. Her eyes grew misty right away, *Here lies a woman who gave her all for love. And what did love give to her in return?*

From the side of her eyes, she saw a girl of about six, wearing a bright dress stop to look at them. She wondered what the kid saw – three adults seeking closure.

Samantha heard the wailing voice of Tashika, shouting for Melissa to forgive her. "Yes, forgive us all, Melissa, for not looking after the only one you loved so much."

# Chapter Twenty-Six

The flight from Bahias de Huatulco Airport in Oaxaca to New York was the hardest for Samantha. Not like there were weather turbulence or technical issues or even faulty human relationship, but Samantha was just not fine. Never had she felt a part of her was left behind leaving a city. But this was her state now.

She couldn't tell if it was boldness or just being resolute, but she made the decision anyway. She made it, despite what Richard thought. He wanted them to return to Aruba to spend a few more days together, to make a definite plan toward becoming a couple, but Samantha insisted it was too early for such plans. He wanted a few more days with her to prepare to live with her absence, but she wasn't going to give in.

"Richard, if I don't leave now, I may never leave again," she had told him, "and I fear I might regret it."

"What do you mean by that? You do not trust me or what?"

Samantha sighed. "Again, I insist it's too soon. It's too soon for everything. It's too soon to talk about trust. Now, do I not trust you? Of course I do, but I do not trust these feelings we share."

Richard was hurt by that. It was written all over his face, the way it fell, like he had been betrayed.

"Don't get me wrong, Richard," she said, "of course, I understand how we feel about each other. It's beautiful, yes. I trust the love we have come to share. What I do not know if it would stand the test of time. Are we just two people who are so broken and are now learning to heal in each other's arm—?"

"And what is wrong with that?"

Actually, there was nothing wrong with healing in each other's arms, Samantha knew. But what would happen after they no longer felt hurt? How would they see each other after they no longer needed to heal and were now whole? She couldn't continue to explain these things to Richard, she was certain he understood, but was too eager to let the moment persist. She could tell he was also scared. He feared she may change, may find out suddenly that she wasn't meant to be with him, and would never consider him anymore. Those were not her intentions.

"I have to go," she said matter-of-factly to Richard. "We need our heads clearer. I mean, you told me you made a mistake with Ash, isn't it right you make your next decision as cautiously as you can?"

Richard said nothing anymore. Two hours' later, he asked her, "Not even your bag? You're not going back to take all your things?"

"I trust you to send them to me," she said.

He understood now that she didn't trust herself enough to leave Aruba once she went back there. The next day, he saw her off to the airport. They stayed in the backseat of Tashika's car, kissing for a long time.

"I told myself I will be fine," Samantha said, "but God knows I will miss us."

Richard smiled sadly. "I will call every day, if you will take my calls."

"I will take them until one of us says enough with this bull-shit."

Richard checked his time. "What's the time for your flight again?"

"2:45."

"Shit! It's 2:40!"

They both literally jumped out of the car and ran like there was a bearded man screaming religious vows in Arabic.

Samantha left.

She was so sad that she was leaving. She knew he felt the same way. She wished he would take another flight and end up in her city the next day. She knew he wouldn't. She tried to think about the future, about her life without him, but she could only think of him.

She had called her mother to tell her she was returning and she had said, "Come straight to me, darling."

She wouldn't go straight to her mother. She needed to wean herself of these feelings she had burning inside her. She knew she couldn't hide it from her mother. The thought of telling her she was in love with Richard haunted her. It was not right. Why Richard? Why did it have to be him that she felt this way about?

"This love didn't have to see the light of the day. It wouldn't," she told herself.

***

Samantha had just finished teaching a class and had returned to her office when her phone rang. It was a video call. Richard was on the line.

Quickly, Samantha adjusted her hair before taking it. "Hey!"

"Sam, baby, why the dry lips? You miss me kissing you?"

"Richard, I seem to remember us agreeing that we would restrict calls till after work hours."

"You do? Oh, me too. But since I am ignoring a board meeting and probably losing about five thousand dollars right now, I think the price of that negligence is adequately compensated."

"There you go with your selfishness. How come what I'm losing by being on this call right now was never included in the count?"

"Oh, my bad. I assumed you'd rather talk to me than do anything else."

"You are deluded." Samantha chuckled. "How are you?"

"Deluded."

Samantha laughed and brushed back strands of hair from her face.

"So, have you spoken to your mum about us yet?"

"No."

"You'll never be able to do this, will you?"

"I will. It's just difficult. I've visited her several times and each time, I just chicken out."

"I remember the first time I wanted to talk to a girl. Each time I got close to her; I took a different path. And then I began seeing her with some girl. I think she waited so long for me and turned lesbian."

Samantha laughed. "If it's your way of encouraging me, its lame."

"I hope you tell her soon, darling, so we can move to other things, like seeing each other again. Jeez, how long has it been?"

"Two months?"

"Just? Let me stop wasting your time, so you can tell her right away."

Samantha smiled. "All right. Take care."

"Love you."

Samantha hung up. She thought about it. She could totally tell her mother right now. She dialed her number and waited, her heart beating.

"Hello, Mum," she said.

"Sammy dear, are you not working?"

"I am. There is something I have to tell you."

# Epilogue

It was the 20th of December. Winter was at its peak. While sitting in the fairly warm flight 347 that was still twenty minutes away from descent, she was ready for the cold that would hug her once she alighted. She didn't want surprises. Richard would be waiting at the airport with a jacket, but she didn't want to become immediately needy.

And what if he surprised her by forgetting a jacket?

The plane hit the runway of the Queen Beatrix International Airport, Oranjestad. Samantha wondered if Richard was watching; if his excitement was building as hers was; if he was going to collapse into her arms or just lift her off the ground. She told herself to not worry about him.

After she cleared her luggage, she strolled to the arrival's unit. Richard surprised her by not being there. She looked around to be sure of this. He wasn't waiting for her. She felt sad. She took her phone, wondering if she was to call him or just call a cab.

She called him.

"I am here, honey," she heard a voice that belonged to Richard say.

She turned around. Richard was there on the floor, kneeling. In his hand was a stone. A shiny stone.

It was an engagement ring.

Samantha's eyes went wild.

"I do not want to ever stay this long without you, baby," Richard said. "Be with me. Live with me. Grow old with me."

Samantha felt her luggage fall off her grip. She was light-headed.

"Marry me, Sam."

Samantha rushed forward and embraced him, going down on her knees with him. Then she kissed him.

"Sam, you're supposed to give me your hand first and then we kiss," Richard said.

Samantha laughed. She stretched her left hand to him.

Richard slipped the ring in the third finger.

Samantha looked at the ring, the stone. It was so beautiful and heart-melting.

"You may kiss me now," she said.

But they were nearly deafened by the roar of the others there. People cheered for them, smiling and laughing, and applauding.

Samantha was shy. The cheering didn't stop.

"Oh well," she said and pressed her lips against Richard's.

They kissed to rapturous applause from their audience. When they stopped kissing, Richard said to her, "I'm ready when you are."

CPSIA information can be obtained
at www.ICGtesting.com
Printed in the USA
BVHW091149260822
645588BV00002B/284